# AND THEN I TURNED INTO A MERMAID

## Laura Kirkpatrick

sourcebooks
young readers

Published by Sourcebooks Young Readers, an imprint of Sourcebooks Kids
P.O. Box 4410, Naperville, Illinois 60567-4410
(630) 961-3900
sourcebookskids.com

Originally published as *And Then I Turned Into a Mermaid* in 2019 in
Great Britain by Egmont, an imprint of Egmont UK Limited.

Library of Congress Cataloging-in-Publication Data is on file with the publisher.

This product conforms to all applicable CPSC and CPSIA standards.

Source of Production: Versa Press, Inc., East Peoria, IL, USA
Date of Production: March 2020
Run Number: 5018024

Printed and bound in the United States of America.
VP 10 9 8 7 6 5 4 3 2 1

*To Millie—*

*my favorite mermaid in the world.*

# Barcastic Barracuda

**M**olly Seabrook loved the sea and hated the sea in equal measure.

She loved it for all the obvious reasons: the gushing and fizzing of waves on the shore, the dolphins leaping during summer, the kaleidoscope of red and orange and pink during sunset.

She hated it because the sea was home to fish. And fish could be caught and battered and served to paying customers in the Seabrook family's fish-and-chip shop where Molly and her sisters were forced to help out. And sometimes, to attract those paying customers, she had to dress up as a *giant haddock*. With fins and everything.

She also hated the sea because her nutty mom was partial to skinny-dipping, which the kids at school absolutely loved to make fun of. Every single lunchtime, without exception, Miranda Seabrook dived into the sea. *Naked.* And every single lunchtime, without exception, Molly was so ashamed that she wanted to roll around in flour and toss herself in the deep-fat fryer just to avoid the pointing and staring.

So again, obvious reasons.

Today, even though it was the end of October, the haddock suit was still hotter than the sun. Trapped in a tomb of polyester scales, Molly was essentially one enormous sweat gland. Salt crystals dripped from her eyebrows and into her stinging eyes. It was nearly the end of her shift, so she looked around for somewhere to ditch her remaining flyers.

She soon found her target. Molly shoved a handful of leaflets into a snotty old lady's canvas shopping bag as she went past. Ordinarily, she would feel bad for reverse pickpocketing, but that same snotty old lady had called the police last week and reported Molly's mom's skinny-dipping. Really, Molly wanted to put an end to her mother's naked antics more than anyone, but having to watch a seaweed-covered Miranda Seabrook being lectured by an angry police officer? While dressed as an oversized fish? Surely, it was more humiliation than any normal human being could handle.

The sun-dappled boardwalk was jammed with tourists sucking on sea marbles—Little Marmouth's famous hard candies. Sea marbles were sweet and tangy and blue, with miniature candy fish inside. Molly hated them on principle.

In fact, right now, she hated most things. She hated the crying toddlers shoving sticky hands into her remaining stash of leaflets. She hated the seagulls cawing overhead in constant poop threat. She hated the gaggle of popular kids from school daring each other to wade waist-deep into the freezing water, squealing and splashing and shrieking, stifling laughs whenever they looked her haddocky way. Most of all, she hated how she wanted to be one of them.

But the Seabrooks had never been popular. After all, popularity isn't easy when you're loud and pushy and always smell like stale deep fryer grease.

Molly lived in a crooked old lighthouse with her four sisters, each more embarrassing than the last, and a mom who liked to feel the sea breeze on her bare skin. Try as she might to fix those things, Molly knew with heartrending certainty that she would never fit in.

Just as she was contemplating hurling the last of her stack of flyers into the sea and abandoning the Good Ship Haddock, her youngest sister, Minnie, darted out of the restaurant and yanked her by the hand. Well, fin.

"Molly-macaroni!" she squeaked, tugging too hard and sending leaflets fluttering all over the boardwalk.

"That nickname makes no sense. It's like me calling you Minnie-lasagna," Molly grumbled, attempting to bend down to retrieve the scattered flyers.

Nobody stopped to help her. Not even Cute Steve, who worked at the ice cream parlor a few doors down. Two years older than Molly, he was the most popular guy in school. And, as the name suggested, incredibly good-looking. In all fairness, at that moment, he was busy scooping mint chocolate chip into a cookie cone for a foot-stomping five-year-old. Molly, who had kind of a thing for Cute Steve, couldn't help but be jealous of the ice cream cone. And the scoop. And the bratty child.

However, Cute Steve barely knew she existed. Considering the weirdness of her family, this was probably for the best.

"Was you being barcastic?" Minnie frowned. "Mom told you not to be barcastic."

"Yes. Barcastic is precisely what I'm being," Molly snapped. "That is absolutely, one-hundred-percent a word."

She was already annoyed at herself for getting annoyed. Her little sister was irritating, which is a serious design flaw in most siblings, but Molly was pretty much Minnie's favorite person in the whole world. The curly-haired, littlest Seabrook was the weirdest of them all, and yet Molly had always had a soft spot for her.

"I thought you was," Minnie snickered. She had Seabrook's famous garlic sauce smeared in her hair like the world's worst glitter gel. "Barcastic barracuda—ha, ha, ha!"

Honestly, barracuda? Molly's sister had an unreasonably thorough knowledge of sea creatures for a five-year-old. Could she spell her own name? No, but she could tell you about the carpet shark in *a lot* of detail.

Molly ruffled Minnie's unruly black hair with her fin. "Whaddaya want, scampi?"

"It's your birfday tomorrow," Minnie said, squirming excitedly in her silver jelly shoes, which Molly noticed were on the wrong feet.

"I am aware, yes. But no fuss, remember? And definitely no fish."

"De-fin-ertly no fish," Minnie confirmed. "De-fin-ertly."

In most families, you probably would not have to say "no fish" when talking about thirteenth birthday plans, but the Seabrooks were not most families.

Not even close.

# CHAPTER
## 2

···············

# A Fishy Birthday

**M**olly awoke on her thirteenth birthday in the bedroom she shared with her sister Melissa in Kittiwake Keep, the converted lighthouse at the end of Little Marmouth pier.

Melissa was fourteen and closest to Molly in age, but Molly got along far better with Margot, who was fifteen and the most gifted practical joker in the northern hemisphere. Molly sometimes wished she could bunk with Margot, but then realized she'd probably wake up with a shaved head and a mouthful of gunpowder, because Margot really liked turning things into cannons.

But back to her birthday. Molly felt both completely different and completely unchanged. The difference was in the crispness of the fresh start. Maybe this would be the year she finally grew out of her mood swings. The year she finally found popularity. The year she finally learned how to spell Egypt.

The unchangedness was in the fish.

Because of course there were fish, despite Minnie's sincere assurances. Every birthday morning in the Seabrook household started with three dozen fish balloons and a giant whale piñata, which the blindfolded birthday girl had to thwack with a sea serpent carved out of driftwood until the whale finally burst and confetti and sea marbles rained down from above.

What was the confetti shaped like?

Fish.

Obviously.

Some birthday traditions were mercifully forgotten. The cardboard conch hat, for example. The spike of the shell had nearly taken Mrs. Figgenhall's eye out last year, which is not how anyone saw the Noah's Ark pageant ending. Mrs. Figgenhall, their religion class teacher, had lost her temper, clutched her eye socket, and wailed that she now knew exactly how Jesus felt when wearing his crown of thorns. Molly thought this was a slight overreaction. In any case, it was mercifully the last time she was cast in any biblical performances.

Finally, Molly escaped the lighthouse and headed to school. Today was the first day back after autumn break, and by the time she had arrived at the Sterling School for Promising Little Marmouthians (SPLuM to its attendees), her birthday was all but forgotten.

Her first class was history, where Molly sat two rows behind Ada, staring at the back of her glossy head. Molly silently willed her best friend to turn around so she could do her evil nun impression. She was willing it so hard that she accidentally forgot to listen to Mr. Hackney droning on about Ancient Greek mythology.

"Ms. Seabrook?"

*Oh no.* Mr. Hackney was looking at her expectantly. "Er, yes, sir?"

"Any ideas?" He smiled warmly, and Molly felt a little guilty for tuning out.

"Sorry, sir, could you repeat the question?"

"At whose ill-fated wedding did the judgment of Paris take place?"

The judgment of what now? Molly forced herself to think of a Greek person, any Greek person, who could reasonably have been getting married twenty billion years ago. "Achilles?"

"Not a bad guess." Mr. Hackney beamed. "It was actually his mother, Thetis."

In that moment, Molly was very grateful for her speedy brain. She'd never tried particularly hard in school—you didn't need straight A's to fulfill a chip-shop destiny—but always managed to pull semidecent grades out of the bag. This made her extremely bright sister, Myla, furious. What was the point of having a brain, Myla said, if you weren't going to use it to cure mumps?

"Thetis was a legendary sea nymph and goddess of the water," Mr. Hackney explained with gusto. "Now, as you all know, Paris choosing who should receive the apple addressed 'to the fairest' sparked the infamous Trojan War..."

Bless Mr. Hackney. He really tried very hard to make his classes interesting, with tales of myths and nymphs and goddesses and others, but everyone knew those things weren't real. Why bother pretending?

At morning recess, she and Ada hid in their favorite locker nook so they wouldn't be forced outside by power-hungry student supervisors. The gap between the lockers and the wall was narrow enough that you couldn't see it from down the hall but big enough to fit two medium-sized thirteen-year-olds and four bags of sour cream and onion potato chips.

Faces inches apart, Ada crunched through three of the four bags while Molly filled her in on the fishy morning she'd had.

"Honestly, Ades, how are we ever going to infiltrate the

popular group when I'm basically one giant fish?" Molly shoved a fistful of chips into her mouth. "And not a cool fish, like a piranha or something. I'm a trout, through and through."

"It's impressive that you're able to eat so many chips, then. Do fish even have teeth?"

Molly frowned. "I feel like I should know, being the daughter of a chip-shop queen."

Ada snorted. "I.e. the worst kind of queen."

Ada had always been a little stuck-up about the chip shop, but Molly just laughed it off—and decided not to tell Margot, who was famous for blowing snot bubbles into the gravy of customers who offended her.

"Did you get to talk to Cute Steve over break?" Ada asked impatiently, as though that was all she really wanted to know.

She and Molly had been swooning over Cute Steve and his best buddy Penalty Pete (who had once scored the winning goal in a school soccer match) for *months*. And since Ada had spent her break at a state park with no phone reception, this was the first chance they'd had for a real debriefing.

Molly puffed out her chest with pride. "Yes. Twice."

"And? What did he say? Did you remember to do that thing we saw on YouTube? Pressing your tongue against the roof of your mouth so you look all pouty and cool?"

"Yes," Molly said vaguely. "Definitely. It went well."

It had not gone well. The video had not been clear on how to talk while midmaneuver, so Molly's words had come out in a garbled warble.

Wiping her crumb-coated hands on her blazer and reaching into her pocket, Ada said, "Anyway. Want your present now?"

Molly, whose mouth was once again full of chips, just nodded excitedly and clapped her hands like a performing monkey.

The gift was small and daintily wrapped in navy paper covered with pretty silver stars. Between the stars, Ada had written in metallic Sharpie, "These are definitely not starfish, you paranoid loon!" but then she'd drawn dangly legs on the stars so they did indeed look like starfish.

Molly chuckled as she tore away the paper to find a fancy lipstick sitting inside. It was so fancy it came in a small cardboard box, which is how you know it's the real deal. Sure enough, the word MAC was stamped proudly on the black packaging. Molly gasped, pulling out the tube. It was a dusty pink color with a glossy finish. It was *gorgeous*.

Ada smirked. "Just to make your trout pout a little less fishy."

"I love it!" Molly threw her arms around Ada, which was

easier said than done in the tiny nook, and she ended up punching the wall with her elbow.

ℓ·ℓ·ℓ

At lunch, while Molly was lining up for hot dogs, Cute Steve was standing right there, right in front of her, black hair flopping attractively. She was so sure he would turn around and say hi, even though he was in ninth grade and much too cool for her. After all, they'd had two whole conversations in the chip shop over school break, both of which had centered around onion rings. What could possibly be more romantic than that?

*And* she had done the tongue-roof thing. She was basically an Instagram model. Was it too late to run to the bathroom and apply a little bit of lipstick?

In any case, Cute Steve was ignoring her. Molly decided to take matters into her own hands. It was hot dog day, so it was the perfect opportunity.

Unfortunately, the second she opened her mouth, the word "glumph" plopped out, like a toad falling into a pond.

However, Cute Steve didn't even notice her sudden transformation into a bullfrog, so that was that.

On Mondays, Ada had band practice during lunch, so Molly usually ate with Melissa and Margot. Today, though,

Melissa had ditched them in favor of the field hockey team she'd recently joined, so it was just Margot and Molly. The way Molly liked it.

However, as Margot chattered away about a new prank she was planning—something to do with birdseed, batteries, and pipe cleaners—Molly found herself envying her older sister's ability to make people laugh. Unlike Molly, Margot was always smiling, always teasing people, always cracking jokes.

Molly wished she had that playful streak. Maybe if she was more like Margot, Cute Steve would suddenly realize that she was the girl of his dreams and immediately kiss her face with his face.

She had no time to dwell on the idea, though, because Margot suddenly looked serious for the first time in her natural-born life. "Hey, it's weird how Myla's leaving, right?"

Molly shrugged. Myla, who was in her final year of Advanced Placement classes, had an interview at Prescott University next month. "She might not get in." Molly knew that wasn't true. Myla would get into NASA if they hired seventeen-year-olds.

"She'll get in somewhere though." Margot stared at her own hot dog with a strange look on her face. Almost...wistful? "Kinda sucks that everything's going to change soon."

Molly was going to protest, to say that it wouldn't change *that* much, but she didn't have the heart to lie to Margot. Since Minnie was born five years ago, there had always been five Seabrook sisters in Little Marmouth. There was no way it wouldn't feel different once Myla left.

Molly vowed then and there to make the most of this birthday, no matter how fishy. After all, it would be the last one they'd all be around for. Things were changing—fast— and soon Molly would look back and wish she'd appreciated her crazy family while they were all still together. Fish and all.

"Love you, Margs," Molly mumbled, fighting the urge to reach over and squeeze her sister's hand.

"That's disgusting," Margot replied and shoved a pipe cleaner up Molly's nose.

# Cake for Dinner

The semicircular kitchen at Kittiwake Keep was a chaotic collection of tables, chairs, and buffets with an ancient, eggplant-colored oven pushed flat against the only straight wall.

The swordfish-printed wallpaper was peeling away. There were windows all around the curve of the lighthouse, so there was always light flooding in. Mom complained about this frequently, since it only served to illuminate the stacks of dirty dishes piled high next to the sink. Their dishwasher had been broken ever since Molly could remember, and their mom never had the cash to fix it.

Tonight, as part of a Seabrook birthday tradition Molly didn't actually mind, the five sisters were making cake for dinner while their mom single-handedly ran the fish-and-chip shop. Since it was Molly's birthday, she got to choose the flavor, and she opted for the same kind she always did: white chocolate and raspberry.

Molly often thought she'd happily drown in melted white chocolate, and she was known for always carrying chocolate with her everywhere she went. The best time for them was in the summer, when they went all gooey and stuck together in one giant blob. Molly enjoyed putting the blob in the fridge to solidify, then gnawing on the entire thing like a beaver with a piece of tree bark.

Since she was the resident expert on the matter, Molly was in charge of melting the white chocolate over the stove, slowly so she didn't burn it, while Myla measured the dry ingredients. Margot and Melissa were blending everything together, and somehow, Minnie had been entrusted with whisking the eggs. The radio on the windowsill blared out a popular song, and the kitchen was warm from the oven's heat.

Myla, the seventeen-year-old supergenius, cleared her throat importantly. "Did you know that it actually wasn't Marie Antoinette who said, 'Let them eat cake'?" Myla mistook the silence for awe, not disinterest. "Honestly, it wasn't! Most people believe she said it on the eve of the French Revolution in 1789, but actually, it was Maria Theresa of Spain, the wife of Louis XIV. She said it a hundred years before Antoinette. Wild, right?"

Molly stifled a laugh as she stirred the glossy chocolate. "Mmm. Wild."

"What do nets have to do with anything?" Margot asked innocently.

Myla stared at her sister as though she were the stupidest person in the whole world. "*Antoinette.*"

Margot met Molly's eye, and they both had to press their lips together to prevent the giggles from escaping. Margot tossed an extra pinch of salt in the batter for good luck.

"Anyone else got any cake trivia?" Myla asked earnestly, oblivious to her sisters' mockery.

Melissa wrinkled her nose as she used a wooden spoon to mix the butter and the sugar together. "This is so unhealthy. For *my* birthday, I want a fruit salad."

"Imagine living in Melissa's head," Molly muttered to Margot. "I bet she wants to ban amusement parks for being too fun."

But Margot didn't hear her, because she'd stuffed a raspberry in each ear to block out the impromptu history lesson.

They popped the delicious white chocolate and raspberry concoction in the oven. While they waited for the magic to happen, they started doing the dishes so their mom didn't have to come home to a messy kitchen. Of course, the kitchen was always messy, so it was a little like rearranging deck chairs on the *Titanic*, but it was the thought that counted.

Molly dunked her finger in the cake-batter bowl. "Hey, remember the time we went to see that unicorn show at the theater for Melissa's birthday?"

"And Minnie stormed the stage?" Margot wrestled the bowl from Molly and shoved her entire face in it to lick the last scraps. Melissa rolled her eyes.

Molly chuckled. "And started kissing the pink unicorn to death."

"Hey!" Minnie said, indignant. "It did not die. Not like Granny Bettie. *She's* dead."

Molly couldn't help it then. Minnie's morbid exclamations made her snort with laughter every time. She was always pointing at stationary objects and insisting they were dead: rocks, streetlamps, Margot during a particularly heavy sleep.

Myla smiled wistfully. "Or what about when Dad was still around and we went bowling? And he...he..."

As Myla trailed off, Melissa shot a worried look at Molly and Margot. Myla was the only one old enough to have any real memories of their father—he left right after Molly was born. Minnie had a different father altogether who wasn't in the picture either. Which meant Myla often felt alone in missing their dad and struggled to talk about him with her sisters.

This made Molly feel a little guilty. What you've never had, you don't miss, and yet it would've been nice for Myla to have someone to share the heartache with. There had always been a kind of distance between Myla and the rest of them, and Molly suspected this was partly why, though there was the whole supergenius thing too. Once, on the plane trip to their one and only foreign vacation in the Caribbean, Molly had asked if it got dark above the clouds. Myla had never looked at her the same since.

"Oh no!" Minnie wailed.

"What is it, scampi?"

"I forgots to put the egg in. Sorry." Sure enough, the semibeaten eggs sat in a bowl over by the broken dishwasher.

"Hey, it's OK, Minnie-moo!" Margot grabbed the bowl and gave it a good stir. "We can put them in now. The cake hasn't been in the oven that long."

"OK." Minnie stared at the ground, tears pooling in her shiny blue eyes. "I'm sorry."

"Stop apologizing, silly." Molly grabbed her by the armpits and hoisted her up onto her hip. It was getting harder to do that now that Minnie was so much bigger, and Molly suspected she'd need a titanium hip replacement by Christmas. "It was a tiny mistake." She ruffled Minnie's hair, which now not only contained garlic sauce but also cake batter, raspberry juice, and several toothpicks from the chip shop.

"See?" Margot said, scraping the eggs on top of the partially baked cake. It had already formed a solid top, which meant she couldn't mix the eggs in correctly with the batter. "It'll be perfect."

This was not convincing in the slightest.

An hour later, the girls were sitting around the wobbly kitchen table forcing down what can only be described as cake topped with burnt omelet. The only one who seemed to be enjoying it was Minnie, who immediately demanded seconds, then thirds. The others found new and inventive hiding places whenever Minnie wasn't looking. Molly really hoped she would remember to retrieve the slab of omelet from the pocket of her school blazer, because the last thing she needed was to be sent out of chemistry for smelling like an eggy fart.

Thankfully, there was soon a knock on the door, and Margot, Melissa, and Molly all dashed out of the kitchen to escape the grossest dinner they had ever had. Molly got to the door first and swung it opened breathlessly.

Eddie of the Ears stood before her, rubbing the back of his neck nervously.

Eddie, whose ears would've looked more at home on a baby elephant, was in Molly's class at school. He was one of the regulars at the chip shop and always ordered the same thing: chips and fried pieces. Molly didn't blame him. Those small, salty scraps of batter scooped from the top of the deep-fat fryer were second only to white chocolate in her eyes.

Clutched in his hand was a large seashell with something painted on the curves.

Margot grinned in disbelief. "Eddie of the...Eddie."

"It's OK," Eddie said, smiling widely. "You can say Ears. Although Eddie of the Eddie has a certain ring to it."

Molly shifted uncomfortably, willing her sisters not to say anything too embarrassing. "What are you doing here?"

Eddie shrugged. "I just wanted to say happy birthday. Because, you know, it's your birthday. And I want you to be happy. Wait, no, that's intense. Er...happy birthday anyway."

He held out the seashell, which had "Happy Birthday Mollie" painted on it in pink and green. It looked a little like a toddler had written it, but it still made Molly feel warm and grateful.

"Thank you, Eddie. That's so sweet."

"Sorry it isn't more," he said, pulling his beanie down so his flaming-red hair wasn't on display. "I don't have a job or anything."

"You can have mine if you want," Molly laughed. "All the free chips and fried pieces you can eat."

"Awesome. They wouldn't even have to pay me."

"Well, that's a relief. They don't pay me either." Molly rolled her eyes. "Getting to live in this lavish mansion is payment enough, my mom figures."

"Do you want to come into our lavish mansion for some cake?" Margot burst out. There was mischief written all over her face, and Molly made a mental scan of the living room for potential booby traps. Definitely a whoopee cushion under the armchair, and almost no condiments in the kitchen were safe.

"What kind of cake?" Eddie asked.

"Scrambled egg," Margot said solemnly. "Toast and bacon are optional."

Eddie looked confused and awkward. "What?"

"Long story," Molly muttered hastily. "Eddie doesn't want to come in, do you, Eddie?"

She actually wouldn't have minded talking with Eddie some more, since he was always pretty funny in the chip shop. But she didn't trust her sisters not to do anything embarrassing, and she certainly didn't trust Minnie not to try to kiss him like the poor pink unicorn.

Eddie, however, looked suddenly crestfallen. "I... No, I guess not. Sorry for bothering you."

"No!" Molly insisted, realizing how awful her rejection

sounded. "You weren't bothering me at all. It's just... My sisters are kind of intense. That's all."

"Rude," said Margot indignantly.

"Don't worry." Eddie smiled. "I get it. See you at school."

Before Molly could protest, Eddie strolled away dejectedly, hands stuffed in his pockets. He climbed into a beat-up old car, which was parked with its headlights on at the end of the street. His mom must've waited to see if he was staying, Molly realized with a pang. He was completely sweet, and she'd totally offended him.

"Margot!" Molly snapped, swirling on her heel. "Why'd you invite him in?"

"What?" Margot held her hands up in mock innocence. "He likes you! God knows why, because you're the absolute worst, but still. He's cute."

"Yes, but our family is not cute. Not in the slightest."

Suddenly rummaging around in her mouth, Margot pulled out a chunk of omelet that she'd stored in her cheek like a hamster, then stuffed it hastily down the back of the battered velvet sofa. "I have no idea what you're talking about."

# The Transformation

That evening, the sky was clear and smattered with twinkling stars. The moon reflected in the smooth surface of the ocean. It was nearly midnight, and the town was fast asleep. And yet, for some absurd reason, here Molly was in a secluded little cove on Little Marmouth beach, shivering in her dolphin-print pajamas.

Less than five minutes earlier, her mom had hauled her out of bed and out of the house. Despite Molly's protests, her mom was adamant and threatened to feed her tuna salad every day for a month if she didn't come along. Like any sane person, Molly detested tuna salad, so here she was.

Now she was left wondering why on God's sandy earth her mom and three older sisters were perching on a cluster of rocks and staring at her so expectantly as she stood at the edge of the water. Minnie had mercifully been left to snooze in the lighthouse mere yards away.

"May I help you?" Molly said. She patted her face to make sure there was nothing on it. The light of her flashlight swung wildly around the cove.

"I wonder what color it's going to be?" Margot chattered excitedly, hopping from one foot to the other. Her long, curly hair was wrapped up in a silk scarf, which she'd stolen from the snotty old lady on the boardwalk.

"It better not be yellow. That's my favorite color." Melissa folded her arms across her chest.

Margot snorted. "Definitely not pink. What's the opposite of pink?"

Myla pushed her glasses up her straight nose. "RGB and CMY are the correct representations of the spectrum of visible light, wherein the opposite of red is cyan, and the opposite of light is dark. Thus, the opposite of light red, aka pink, is dark cyan, aka teal."

Margot smirked. "Or...pinkn't."

A wave crashed and fizzed on the sand, narrowly missing Molly's feet. The tide was coming in.

Molly was getting more irritated with every nonsensical comment. "What are you talking about, for the love of—"

"Less of the lip, Molly," her mom tsked. Thankfully, she

was fully clothed this evening, which was a relief for every-one. "And for what it's worth, my money's on tangerine."

Molly pressed her teeth down on her tongue to stop the snarky comment from escaping. But just then, another wave lapped at the shore, at Molly's feet, and the tips of her toes began to tingle.

She blinked against the moonlight, wiggling her toes in her now too-tight rubber boots. The tingle continued to spread, a confusing warmth building in the arches of her feet, shooting up the planes of her shins, and wrapping around the crooks of her knees.

*Am I having a stroke?* she wondered, terror growing in her chest.

Her great-uncle had a stroke once, back when Molly was in elementary school. Apparently, he smelled burnt toast when it happened. Molly sniffed the air in desperation, trying to pick up a trace of charred whole wheat bread, but all that met her nostrils was the tangy stench of seaweed. And, you know, seagull poop.

"What's happening to m—" she started before realiz-ing her discomfort was causing excitement levels among her siblings to skyrocket. The more her legs shook like jelly, the more they grinned and squealed. "Seriously, why—*Ooft!*"

Suddenly, her legs clamped together, causing Molly's

balance to be entirely thrown off. She fell backward and hit the sand with a muffled thud, eyes watering from the impact. As she did, her loudmouthed family fell deadly silent.

"Can someone help me up?" Molly moaned, massaging the spot on her shoulder that had taken the brunt of the fall. Nobody moved. "Or, you know, don't, and just watch me suffer."

Still silence.

Her hip was aching too. Molly went to rub it and let out a squeal.

It felt like...scales?

Molly gasped, wiggling into the best sitting position she could manage. She was terrified to look down, but her eyes tugged her there anyway.

No. Impossible. She had a *tail*.

A mermaid's tail, whiter than snow.

She was dreaming. She had to be. Or was it an elaborate practical joke? Margot *was* famous for her pranks, and this was a particularly impressive one. Next, she'd be turning Cute Steve into a centaur. Molly didn't think she'd mind that, actually. She'd always thought centaurs were weirdly handsome.

"Very funny, Margot," she said, trying to find the place where the tail ended and her waist began so she could wrench the darn thing off. But even in the starlight, Molly could see that Margot was pale as the moon, lips pressed into a faint pink line. And most notably, Margot also had a tail. Fire-engine red and speckled with coppery sparkles.

In fact, they all did. Mom, who was now paddling in a rock pool, had a tail of dreamy lavender. Melissa's was buttercup yellow, and Myla's was deep emerald green with silver shimmers.

Really, this was a very advanced practical joke. Molly had to applaud Margot. She had definitely evolved from the days of plastic wrap over the toilet seat.

She was about to congratulate her sister on her world-class pranking abilities when something stopped her in her tracks. Her hand had found the place where the tail joined her waist, high up near her belly button, but there was no seam. It was like the scales were welded to her skin. Like they really were a part of her.

The thought sent her stomach into a spiral, and dizzy spots prickled around her vision.

"Um, guys? What's going on?" she asked.

Myla was the first to speak. "It's white. That's…different."

"That's *boring*," Melissa added.

Margot snorted. "When it's Minnie's turn, I'm starting an official sweepstakes, and I'm putting all my worldly possessions on mauve."

Molly felt four pairs of eyes boring into her, like when

the seagulls watch you intently in case you drop some food. She still felt dazed and woozy, the way she did when she was drifting off to sleep.

Forcing some strength into her voice, she muttered, "If you're done with your nonsense commentary, I have some questions."

"Right! Yes, of course," said Mom, wiggling her pale purple tail in the rock pool. "What would you like to know?"

Molly stared at her. "Well, I thought that might be obvious."

"Well, we thought the mermaid thing might be obvious," Margot snarked back.

Molly shot her a dagger-filled glare.

Shuffling up onto a rock, her mom said gently, "You're half mermaid, sweetie."

"Half?"

"Your dad was a regular human."

Molly never thought she'd envy her long-lost father for something as basic as his biology. "Lucky him."

Mom ignored the snark. "Anyway, now that you're thirteen, your mermaid side has awoken. You're old enough to explore the other part of your life. Your tail. Your mermaid-hood. But *don't* go in the deep sea. It's no longer safe. *Especially* for half humans."

"Oh, right, of course," Molly muttered. "No sea. I'll just

flop around on the boardwalk, then. How about ponds? Are ponds dangerous? Or swamps?"

"Ponds are fine," Mom answered as though it had been a serious question. "I wouldn't recommend swamps."

Molly's mind raced. Surely, *surely*, she was dreaming. And yet when she bit down hard on her tongue, she didn't wake up. Her chest pounded, and her breathing grew quicker and quicker as she tried to fight back the tide of panic.

"But mermaids aren't real," she said, her words growing in uncertainty the more she examined her bright white tail. "They... We... Mermaids aren't *real*."

"That's what we want them to think," Mom replied, winking.

*Who's "them"?* Molly wondered as she stared at her shimmering scales. The tail was as easy to move and control as her legs and twice as powerful.

Looking around at her sisters, Molly noticed they weren't wearing those tacky seashell bras like mermaids do in cartoons. Instead, they were wearing elegant long-sleeved tops—perfectly fitted and cropped just above their tails, in the same shimmery colors as their scales—that they definitely had not left the house in. Even her mom, who'd had a double mastectomy not long after Minnie was born, wore a top so well-fitting it was like her very own skin had turned a glittering lavender purple. Molly looked down to find her own pajama top had somehow been replaced with a beautiful, shimmering white top.

Molly dimly wondered how all their pajamas and shoes had disappeared, but it seemed pretty minor compared to suddenly sprouting a fish tail, so she shook the thought away.

"I'm... I'm a mermaid?" she said, as though saying it out loud would make it feel more real.

"But you only get the tail when you're near water," Margot explained, adjusting her scarf. Her poppy-colored tail was vivid and, Molly had to admit, beautiful.

"How near?" Molly asked.

"When you can feel the ocean in your heart, then you're near enough," murmured Mom, eyes glazed and glassy.

"Right, fantastic," Molly snapped. "In my heart. Got it. But just as a rough estimate, how many yards?"

"The mermaid instinct cannot be measured in yards," her mom answered, laying her hand over her heart. "There's no tape measure for the soul."

Molly tried again. "Right, but if there *were* a tape measure for the soul, what might it say? Like, am I going to flop around the school hallways whenever it rains outside? Am I going to knock people out with my flailing tail whenever we pass the swimming pool?"

Mom nodded. "If your soul desires it."

Molly had the strong urge to slap her mother with a wet cod but figured there was every chance mermaids enjoyed that sort of thing.

"Mom's mastered it to the extent where she doesn't transform until she's actually *in* the water. It's very impressive."

"Hence the skinny-dipping," Margot added with an eye roll.

"How is this happening?" Molly whispered fearfully, a thousand questions simmering in her brain.

"How does anything happen?" Mom answered. "It just…is."

"So if Minnie came home one day with an elephant trunk, you'd say, oh, never mind, it just is?"

Margot snorted. "Be realistic, Molly."

"Realistic! You call this thing *realistic*?"

Myla tutted, shaking her head. "You're really being very closed-minded."

"Well, excuse me for not just immediately being like, oh, I have a tail, cool, what's for dinner?"

"We already had dinner," Margot pointed out. "It was awful."

"Oh my God, why are you deliberately dodging my questions?"

Mom snapped out of her sea-witch whisper and sighed. "Molly, if you'd just calm down—"

Anger bubbled in Molly's throat. "How do you honestly expect me to calm down?"

Melissa inhaled deeply, then exhaled exaggeratedly. "Just...breathe." She looked up at Mom for approval.

"Through what, my face or my gills?" Molly snapped. "Assuming I have gills? For the whole breathing underwater thing?" Running her hands over her once smooth neck, sure enough, there was a set of gills. "Great. Just what I've always wanted. Holes in my skin! The hot new look! Coming to a freak show near you!"

Even Margot looked worried now, wringing her hands together and gritting her teeth. "Molly, seriously, can you please just relax?"

"I'll relax *you*!" Molly shouted. "Permanently! You know, because you'd be *dead*."

"Molly!" her mom yelled, raising her voice for the first time in forever, at the same time as Margot said, "That's a little much."

Molly wasn't about to stick around to be told off. She began shuffling up the beach as best she could, using her hands to drag her impossibly heavy tail through the wet sand. Gasping and panting, Molly cursed this stupid situation as she moved mere inches at a time while her mother and sisters watched with alarm—and a little amusement.

She'd gone no farther than two yards when she finally gave up, collapsing on the ground with a sob.

Mom shuffled over to the spot where Molly lay facedown in the sand and rubbed her shoulder affectionately. Her palm was warm and soft and comforting. "Molly, talk to me. Why is this upsetting you so much?"

"Because...because..." Molly spluttered, mouth full of sand. "I'm a *freak*. We're all freaks. We always have been, and now we're even more so. Why can't I—we—just be *normal*?"

"There will come a time when you're grateful for the things that make you stand out. Trust me. Until then, you just have to weather the storm. And you're a Seabrook— we've always been good at weathering storms." Mom gestured to her flat chest, then her empty ring finger, and smiled warmly.

Molly did understand what Mom was saying, but all she could muster was a half-hearted "Hmph."

"And you mustn't tell a single soul, all right? This is a secret we will take to the grave. Not a single soul. Do you understand?"

Molly snorted then. Did her mom think she was some kind of idiot? Like she'd ever tell *anyone* how much of a freak she really was.

And that was it. The truth bigger than all of this. Bigger

than discovering her freakish family were in fact mermaids. Bigger than having her very own tail.

Cute Steve would never be interested in her now.

And she would never, ever be popular. Not in a million years.

# So Many Questions

After they'd crawled far enough away from the sea to transform back into humans, Molly finally caught her breath and focused on one thing and one thing only: getting out of this cove.

When they got back to Kittiwake Keep, everyone went to their bedrooms, somehow in the very clothes they'd worn down to the beach. Molly's mind reeled. She had a million questions about the mermaid deal, and the pajama situation was near the top of the list.

However, when they got to their room, Melissa seemed intent on lecturing Molly rather than answering her many questions.

"You know, you really shouldn't speak to Mom like that, Molly." Melissa perched on her side of her bed, arms folded across her nightgown. "You can be very hurtful at times. I know this is all a shock, but there's no need to be so...*Molly* about it."

Through gritted teeth, Molly muttered, "Yep. Got it. Don't be who I am. Excellent."

Melissa sighed and lay down, shutting the light off.

Molly's entire body was shaking as she got under the covers. It wasn't from cold, she didn't think, although it had been bitter down on the beach—just adrenaline and shock and the urge to laugh and cry and scream and do a weird little dance all at the same time.

How could she possibly fall asleep now? There were so many thoughts whizzing through her head and nobody to talk them through with. She'd been too shocked to speak on the walk back to the lighthouse, but now she was buried under the weight of her questions. She would gladly be turned into a cannon if it meant being able to talk with Margot. Unfortunately, she had to share a room with an unsympathetic Goody Two-shoes, who Molly would really like to shove—

There was a tap on the door. Several taps, in fact. One long one, three short ones, and another long one.

The secret knock.

Margot.

Molly smiled gratefully into the darkness. The door creaked open, and sure enough, Margot padded through in her squid-print bathrobe, lighting the way with the flashlight on her phone. She then swiveled around and did a moonwalk the rest of the way to Molly's bed. Melissa sighed extravagantly, as though she were the queen of England and someone had just peed on her corgi.

"How you doing, Mol?" Margot whispered, perching on the end of Molly's bed and awkwardly patting her foot through the duvet.

"I'm—"

Just then, there was another tap on the door. Margot and Molly stared quizzically at each other. The door creaked open once again, and this time, Myla's head appeared through the crack.

"Room for a big one?" she mumbled, and Molly had to fight the urge to burst into tears. It had been so long since Myla had come to her bedroom for a talk, and she hadn't realized how much she'd missed it until now.

"Yes," Molly sniffed, trying to swallow the emotion as best she could.

The three sisters squished together on Molly's bed, Melissa glaring at them from across the room.

"Are you joining us, your royal highness?" asked Margot.

Melissa looked like she desperately wanted to join in, but she was still mad at Molly for being Molly. "No, I'll just stay here."

Molly half wished Minnie would shuffle over in her too-long jammies and snuggle between them all, but then she remembered the garlic sauce in her hair and thought better of it. She wasn't really in the mood to smell like a pizza.

Minnie. On the one hand, Molly was sad she'd have to keep this huge secret from her baby sister until she, too, turned thirteen. But on the other hand, if Minnie knew, she would probably treat Molly like a giant sea turtle and constantly demand rides in the water.

Molly wondered how each of her other sisters had reacted when they first learned about the mermaid thing. Margot had taken it best, she guessed, and would've immediately started to plan the millions of new pranks she could play. Molly couldn't even imagine how many intellectual questions Myla must've asked. Melissa... Melissa was a teacher's pet. She'd probably started planning ways to impress Mom by being the best mermaid ever.

"It's not as bad as you think, Mol." Margot shuffled the duvet so it covered them all equally. "The mermaid stuff. Once you get used to it, it's actually pretty fun."

"You think everything's fun," Molly pointed out. "You had a whale of a time when we last went to the dentist."

"Oh come on, you can't tell me that slobber-sucking machine isn't hilarious."

"Is that why you held banana milkshake in your mouth, and then when the machine drank it up, you patted it and said, 'Was that tasty, little guy?'"

Margot almost wet herself from laughing. Unable to fight off the snickers, Molly started giggling too. Myla rolled her eyes. "You guys are ridiculous."

Molly's laughter died as quickly as it had started. She chewed her lip. "I just don't understand how we're supposed to go about our normal lives with this enormous...*thing* hanging over us."

"You're thinking about it the wrong way," Myla said quietly. "It's not hanging over you. It's deep inside you. It's the thing you carry with you that lets you know you're special."

Even though her stomach was still in knots, it was a comforting thought. Molly had never had something particularly special about her before. Not like Myla's intelligence or Melissa's moral compass or Margot's humor or Minnie's zest for life. And yet, if she shared her special thing with her entire family, did that really make *her* special at all?

Still, it was nice to have something connecting them. They were all such different people, and this was a common thread between them. Molly already felt closer to them somehow.

"You're not alone, Mol," Margot said. "We're all in this together. And the mermaid community is so great. You're going to love old Alan. He's this ancient merman with—"

"Wait, *what?*" Molly gasped. "There are other mermaids here? In Little Marmouth?"

Myla nodded solemnly, lowering her voice to a whisper. "The legend goes that there used to be a grand mermaid queendom called Meire, but humans filled the sea with so much plastic and other garbage, oil spills and extreme amounts of sewage—"

"*Poop*," Margot added slowly, as though Molly were an idiot.

Melissa tutted in the corner. "That's disgusting."

"Yes, feces, excrement, whatever you want to call it," Myla muttered impatiently. "It's dumped in the sea, making it no longer safe for mermaids to live down there, so they moved up to the shore."

"All of them?" Molly asked, suddenly feeling extremely guilty about using the bathroom and not recycling her juice cartons as often as she should.

*Wait, how do mermaids use the bathroom?*

Myla shrugged. "Most of them, yes, to seaside towns all around the world. Including Little Marmouth."

This piqued Molly's interest. "Wow, OK. So who else in this town is a mermaid? Come on, dish the dirt."

"*Fish* the dirt," Margot corrected. She cracked her knuckles. "OK. Bertha Henderson, who owns the amusement arcade on the boardwalk, and her husband. I forget his name. Long beard, like a goat or something. They've got a kid in elementary school, I think. Oh, and Andy Miller in tenth grade. He's a good guy. Impressive spear. Who else...? Amy Fairbairn, who's a senior—her family owns the butcher's."

"Is she really a mermaid?" Myla blinked, looking genuinely surprised. "I'd never noticed."

"That's because she's not a walking science textbook," Margot answered.

Myla rolled her eyes, but this time, there was a hint of a smile on her usually serious features.

"Is that everyone?" Molly asked.

"There are a few more. No one else from school, though." Margot smiled. "But the point is, Mol, you're not alone. OK? You have us."

"*All* of us." Myla squeezed Molly's hand. "Right, Melissa?"

"All of us," Melissa said in a small, sheepish voice, right before Margot threw a stuffed alligator at her head.

# CHAPTER
# 6

# The First Hurdle(s)

The next morning, Molly might've thought the whole thing had been a very strange dream. She wished it *had* been a dream, but that was impossible, because she hadn't had a single wink of sleep.

As she got dressed for school, she had a sick feeling in her stomach, like she'd eaten some bad fish. Not because none of this felt real—in fact, it was just the opposite, like a part of her had always known. Like she had always been building to this moment.

It...made sense.

That didn't make it any easier to bear, though. The mermaid thing made her even more of a freak and outcast than she already was. Did her genes not know she had a handsome fifteen-year-old with floppy hair to attract? The odds were already against her, since she was thirteen and a nobody. And she didn't think there were any YouTube tutorials on how to hide a fish tail from the man of your dreams, but maybe she just needed to look harder.

Then there was the *whiteness* of the tail. Everyone else had a gorgeous color, and hers was plainer than plain could be. It made her feel like even more of a nobody than ever— the least exciting member of the world's weirdest family.

In any case, Molly vowed not to return to the beach anytime soon. The whole thing had left her even more at odds with herself than the time Margot had replaced her shampoo with blue hair dye (although being sent home from math class to wash it out *was* something of a victory).

That morning at school passed by in a haze of exhaustion. When she first bumped into Ada at their lockers, she felt like she had a neon sign flashing above her head, exposing her secret. Certainly, there was no *way* Ada wouldn't notice this fundamental change in her best friend? But Ada seemed totally oblivious, which was fine by Molly. She was in no rush to share her very special brand of weird with the world. Even if keeping secrets from her best friend *did* leave her feeling kind of gross.

For the next few hours, Molly was so exhausted, she could barely prop her eyelids open. She kept walking around with them closed while Ada steered her around various obstacles. Which worked well until Ada became distracted by Penalty Pete dribbling a soccer ball down the hall, and Molly collided nosefirst with a disgruntled Mrs. Figgenhall. The religion class teacher squawked like a constipated gibbon. It was like the conch hat incident all over again. Molly felt a little bad and vowed to purchase Mrs. Figgenhall a motorcycle helmet as an apology. And also possibly to look into nose reduction surgery as an act of public service.

History was a snooze fest of epic proportions, and chemistry was a confusing blur of numbers and symbols Molly had no hope of understanding. Honestly, what kind of medieval torturer came up with the periodic table?

Still, before she knew it, she was sitting with Margot and Melissa at lunch again. Ada was at choir practice, which made Molly consider getting a new best friend with fewer wholesome hobbies, but at least she had an opportunity to ask some of the many questions that had been bubbling over in her brain since the previous night.

Stretching her arms in the air, Molly stifled a yawn and whispered, "So what's the deal with mermaid peeing?"

"Molly!" Melissa snapped. "Remember what Mom told you! We can't talk about that at school. Not *ever*. Do you understand me? We could get in so much trouble! Nobody can know. *Nobody.*" She shook her head gravely, as though Molly were some sort of criminal. "I'm going to eat with my friends."

And with that, Melissa flounced away toward the other Goody Two-shoes she hung around with. As she walked past Felicity Davison from eighth grade, Molly saw Felicity mime holding her nose. Her fellow Populars laughed meanly.

Molly felt a familiar flash of anger. Melissa might be annoying, but she was still Molly's sister, and it was horrible seeing someone make fun of her. Especially someone like Felicity Davison, who had the whole of SPLuM at her feet.

*Note: feet. Like, permanently. Never tail.* Molly never thought that was something she'd have to be jealous of.

Trying to shake away the anger at Felicity, Molly flashed an eye roll at Margot, like she usually did whenever Melissa mounted her high horse. To her surprise, though, Margot looked sheepish.

"Melissa's actually right, Mol." Margot chewed her lip. "We could get in real trouble with the government if this secret gets out."

"Mmm, yes, I'm sure this is exactly the kind of thing the president gets involved in," Molly replied drily, taking a bite of baked potato.

Margot snorted. "Not the human government, you idiot."

"Ah. The schmermaid government, then."

Margot raised an eyebrow. "Schmermaid?"

"Just in case anyone overhears us."

"Oh yes. Your code is truly brilliant. Truly impossible to decipher. They could really use you over at the FBI. And yes, the schmermaid government."

Molly laughed so hard, she spat cheese everywhere. "They have a government? Where's Congress? Rock pool thirty-six in never-never land?"

Margot looked genuinely hurt. "Democracy isn't just for legged species, you know."

Holding up her hands, Molly sighed. "Fine. You win. No schmermaid talk at school."

However, it was only a matter of hours before Margot broke her own rule. She passed Molly in the hallway as they were both coming from fifth period and nodded toward the giant bottle of iced tea in Molly's hands.

"Better be careful with that," Margot whispered darkly.

"What? Why?"

"Anything over a liter is a transformation risk."

"Are you making fun of me?" Molly muttered.

Margot shrugged. "Go on, then. Find out the hard way."

Molly hastily shoved the iced tea back in her backpack, ignoring Ada's quizzical looks.

Later, though, she realized Margot must have been joking. Just last week, she'd walked in on Melissa having a bath, and even though it was pretty shallow, it was certainly more than a liter full. Melissa had shrieked for Molly to get out while she slathered hair removal cream all over her legs and, more entertainingly, her mustache area. Molly had told Margot this, and her older sister made an effort to always have some kind of mustache on her own face when Melissa entered the room. Her favorite props were string cheese, chocolate mousse, and pepperoni.

Foolishly, Molly seemed to think that she had managed to avoid a catastrophe for today, so she wasn't paying attention when she stopped by the bathroom before she walked home. She ignored the yellow "CAUTION: WET" sign taped to the front of the door and pushed her way into the girls' bathroom without a second thought.

Right into an enormous pool of water from a flooded toilet.

Slipping on a wad of soggy toilet paper, Molly tumbled to the ground.

Almost at once, the tingling started, and she felt her legs clamping together.

*NO!*

Panic set in as she tried to struggle to her feet, but she

just ended up flailing madly and coating the walls and ceiling in the spilled water.

*Maybe if I make it back into the hallway before I fully transform...*

But she wasn't moving fast enough. Her uniform disappeared, and her pale skin turned into even paler white scales. Her blazer made way for the shimmery white top. Fighting the urge to scream and yell, Molly grabbed her phone from her backpack and texted Margot.

Schmermaid emergency! First-floor bathroom! HELP OR YOU ARE NO LONGER MY SISTER!!

Thrashing around so violently it was like she was being electrocuted, Molly tried to control her panic, but it was no use. The mere sight of her ghostly white tail was enough to send shivers up her spine.

*Oh God, oh God, oh God. What if the custodian finds me here at midnight? What if I've become so desperate she finds me sawing my own tail off with a plastic ruler?*

Praying that Margot didn't take too long with her marine rescue, Molly decided to take matters into her own hands. She tried to turn over, but her tail just flapped uselessly from side to side. When she attempted to drag herself to the door, she found that the flooded floor was too slippery for her hands, and she just ended up face planting into the tile.

Why had the tail seemed so much easier to control on the beach? Maybe she was getting too worked up. *Breathe, Molly.*

Time for plan B.

Rubbing her nose, which had now been bruised twice in the space of one school day, she gripped the lip of a sink and tried to haul herself up out of the shallow water.

Unfortunately, her upper-body strength was almost nothing, and she collapsed to the ground with an *oomph*. The impact caused her to burp very loudly.

Again and again, she tried to lift herself up from the floor using the sink, hoping a dry tail might become legs once more, and again and again, she flopped back down and burped involuntarily.

*Right, I need a new tactic*, she thought, gritting her teeth.

Molly's next idea was to invent some sort of pulley system. Her backpack was now saturated with water and very heavy. Plus, the straps were really long. Maybe if she could toss the heavy part over the top of the stall while clinging on to the strap, it would act like one of those spiky things on a long rope that cartoon spies use to get into high buildings.

Gathering all the strength she had—and wishing she had paid more attention when Mr. Hopkins had tried to teach them javelin—Molly launched the backpack with all her might. Unfortunately, she overdid it somewhat...and forgot to hold on to the straps. The backpack landed directly in the toilet with a *plop*.

Despairingly, Molly wondered why she couldn't throw half that well during basketball. Because she was taller than average, she was always the shooting guard—where she proceeded to make a total and utter idiot of herself.

There was still no sign of Margot. With desperation now mounting, Molly tried one more time to haul herself out of the gross mini lake using the sink.

With an enormous crack, the sink severed itself from the wall in a dusty splintering of plaster. Molly fell backward, still holding on to the sink, and was almost immediately crushed beneath it.

Well, crushed was an exaggeration. Molly's body was stuck in the crook of the sink, where the bowl met the stem, so she was not actually in any physical danger. But still, she was wedged in there pretty tightly and at the complete mercy of whoever walked in next.

What if Ada came looking for her? Or even worse, Felicity Davison and her popular squad? What would they find? A beached whale trapped beneath a gross sink, suffering the world's worst shower from a burst pipe.

In a long-overdue piece of good luck, Margot *was* the next person through the door. Phone in hand, she took one look at Molly and erupted into the deepest belly laugh of all time.

On and on and on the laughing went. Honking like a startled goose, Margot clutched the one remaining upright sink.

"How?" she asked, completing her own transformation into a schmermaid. "Just... Oh my actual God, Molly! *How?*"

Molly would have folded her arms indignantly had she not been pinned to the ground by a giant chunk of porcelain. "Just help me up, would you? Maybe if you drag me out from one side..."

Once she'd finally caught her breath and wiped away the tears of laughter streaming down her freckly face, Margot grabbed the sink with one hand and effortlessly lifted it off the ground and Molly.

Molly stared at her as Margot propped it back against the wall. "Mind explaining how you're some kind of powerlifter?"

Margot shrugged as though she'd done nothing more impressive than pick up a pencil. "It's my merpower."

"Merp-what? What's a merp hour? I have never heard of the verb 'to merp.'"

"Mer*power*. Every mermaid has one." Margot stuck her head into the hallway to make sure the coast was clear, then effortlessly pulled Molly through the toilet lake until they were back on dry floor. "Mine is super strength."

"Margot, I watched you struggle to open the tumble dryer the other day."

Margot wiggled her fire-engine-red tail. "Only when I have this thing. Otherwise, I'd be on all those weird TV shows where people have to pull trucks for no reason."

Relief flooded through Molly as her legs—and somehow her tights and skirt—reappeared. Then came her blazer and shirt. She rested her soaking back against the hallway wall and sighed. "What's mine, then? When do you find out? Is there some kind of welcome-to-mermaidhood ceremony I need to attend?"

Margot busied herself with retrieving Molly's backpack from the bathroom. Calling back out into the hallway, she said, "Mmm, yes, they push you out into the Atlantic on a wooden raft, and if you make it all the way to Portugal, you're officially a mermaid. That is where the verb 'to merp' comes from."

"Margot..."

Margot dumped the soggy backpack next to Molly and wiped her hands on her blazer as her own legs returned. "You just kind of...find out. Mine didn't take long, obviously. Soon as I picked up a speedboat with my left thumb, I thought something was a little off. And Melissa can tell when people are lying. That didn't take long either, since I lie to her roughly seventeen times per day."

*What will my merpower be?* Molly found herself wondering, although part of her was scared of the answer. What if it was something as boring as her white tail?

"What about Myla?" she asked.

"Hers took forever to discover. She can speak every sea language without having to study them. Well, with the exception of Kelpish, but that's only spoken in rivers and streams."

"Oh, well, of *course* not Kelpish!" Molly snorted. "That would be absurd!"

Margot pulled a piece of string cheese out of her blazer pocket and shoved the entire thing in her mouth at once. Molly wished she had a piece of white chocolate to gnaw on. "Kind of a pointless merpower, since we no longer live in the sea. Myla being Myla, she uses it to study ancient aquatic texts."

Molly thought she wouldn't know an ancient aquatic text if it kicked her in the head, but good for her sister.

In any case, she couldn't wait for the day this all felt normal to her too.

# The Embarrassing Friend

The toilet lake was just the beginning.

The next week, there were a lot of newfound problems to contend with. During their swimming lesson, Molly not only had to make her excuses as to why she had to sit this one out—she was surprised Mr. Hopkins bought the tuberculosis explanation—but she also had to make sure she was far enough away from the water that she wouldn't spontaneously transform into a mermaid. The second she felt scales forming on her hips as they walked to the pool, she knew she was in danger of transforming and set herself up in the cafeteria with a raspberry-ice slushie—that well-known cure for late-stage tuberculosis.

The one plus side of wearing a haddock suit to work was that if Molly didn't notice the tide had come in and was lapping at the foot of the boardwalk, her sudden and severe transformation was disguised by the layers of cheap polyester.

The downside was that she couldn't stretch out her arms in the suit's tiny fins, so every time the tail sent her tumbling to the ground, she had no way of breaking her fall. She had been to the doctor twice in the space of a week, once with a sprained wrist and once with a suspected concussion. The doctor gravely advised her to give up contact sports.

Molly wished it were that simple. Being a part-time mermaid was, frankly, a little inconvenient.

However, she and Ada were making some slight progress on their mission to infiltrate the Populars and convince Cute Steve and Penalty Pete to pay attention to them.

They were hiding in their locker nook one day, chowing down on barbecue potato chips, when Ada excitedly whispered, "You'll never guess what!"

"Mermaids are real and walk among us?" Molly suggested.

Ada snorted. "Yeah, like mermaids can walk."

Molly nodded sagely. "Good point."

"So, Penalty Pete spoke to me!"

"Oh my God, really?" Molly felt genuinely excited for her friend, who had loved Pete since long before his penalty-shoot-out fame. "What did he say?"

"I stopped by the soccer field after band practice, just to watch him play for a while. Build up the face recognition, you know?"

Molly nodded again, dipping her finger into the crumbs at the bottom of the packet and sucking off the last smidge of flavor. She then dug into her pocket for her packet of chocolate. "Planning long-term strategy. Smart."

"Exactly." Ada screwed her face up. "Ugh, Felicity Davison was there too, though, waving flirtily at Cute Steve."

Molly's stomach sank. "Did you kick her in the shins?"

Ada was not at all shocked by or concerned with this question. "Yep. Twice on each leg."

"Attagirl."

"Then someone kicked the ball out of bounds, and it landed near me, so I picked it up."

"And?"

"Penalty Pete jogged over, so I passed it back to him, and he said, 'Thanks.' Then he looked at my tuba and said, 'What's that?' and I said, 'It's a tuba, Pete.' And he said, 'Cool,' and ran away again." Ada's face was practically glowing at this point. It was like looking at an ultraviolet light. "Can you *believe* it? He now knows about my tuba!"

To Molly, this didn't sound anywhere near as romantic as the conversation she and Cute Steve had held about onion rings, but she didn't want to dash Ada's dreams. "Ada, do you know what I think? I think you've basically been to first base."

This was only accurate if there were six thousand bases after that one, but still. Tuba banter had to mean *something*.

Turns out it did. Over the following few weeks, Ada managed to manufacture several more mindless conversations with the soccer star turned tuba fan. The brief talks were going better and better, to the point where Penalty Pete actually learned Ada's name and actively smiled whenever he saw her.

For some reason, though, Molly noticed Ada didn't want her around during these wooing attempts. She kept making half-hearted excuses about choir and band and headaches and family emergencies and would only later tell Molly about another instance of Pete communication.

One day, Molly waited in the locker nook for twenty minutes at morning recess, but Ada never showed up. While this was positive in that Molly got to eat four packages of Lay's herself, it was still irritating.

They didn't have the next class together, since Ada was in AP English, and by the time lunch rolled around without an apology text, Molly was beginning to feel a little annoyed and abandoned.

When Ada dumped her lunch on the table and plonked down next to Molly, Molly barely looked up.

"What's wrong?" Ada said immediately.

"Nothing."

"Why aren't you looking at me?"

"I don't know. Do I normally look at you?"

"Yes, Molly. You're like a googly-eyed bat."

"Bats are blind. Honestly, aren't you meant to be in the advanced classes?"

Ada looked affronted. "Seriously, what's gotten into you?"

Molly's cheeks burned red like they always did when she was frustrated. She stabbed at her baked beans with a knife. "You just keep dumping me to spend time with Penalty Pete. I don't understand why I can't come with you when you speak to him. Doesn't he think it's weird that you're always by yourself?"

Shrugging, Ada bit into her peanut butter and jelly sandwich, which Molly knew she only ate because she saw all the popular kids eating them. "I think he thinks I'm really independent. Mysterious, you know? I need to seem mature enough for him—he is two years older, after all."

Molly lowered her voice, not wanting to sound petulant. "And you don't care that you're leaving me by myself?"

"You're not by yourself!" Ada replied overenthusiastically. "You have your sisters, don't you?"

Molly knew Ada was deliberately missing the point, so she said nothing.

"Come on, Mol." Ada licked rogue jam from the side of her mouth. Molly noticed her lips were painted with nude lipstick. "This was always our game plan! We infiltrate the Populars, start going out with Pete and Steve, and then when we're grown up, we buy houses next door to each other so all our kids can be friends. Have you changed your mind?"

Thinking of Cute Steve's floppy hair—and also the idea of him as a centaur—Molly muttered, "No," even if half-mermaid, half-centaur babies did seem impossible.

"So there's no problem," Ada announced with an air of finality. "We're right on track."

That was when Molly started to feel a little relieved that she couldn't tell Ada about the mermaid thing—not even if she wanted to. Knowing the truth would probably make her ever more embarrassed to be seen with Molly, especially if she started going out with Penalty Pete for real.

However, despite all Molly's best efforts to behave as normally as possible, Ada turned out to be ashamed of her anyway.

A few days later, Molly was walking to history after morning recess when she overheard Ada talking to Penalty Pete and Felicity Davison by the water fountain. Ada had hiked her skirt up shorter than usual and had styled her glossy black hair in the same way all the popular girls wore it at the moment—half-up, half-down, with thin braids wrapping around the side.

"...this one time, *I had to rescue my friend's mom from jail*," Ada was saying.

Molly stopped in her tracks, the sinking feeling in her stomach telling her exactly where this was going.

Felicity, the queen bee of eighth grade, coiled a lock of smooth blond hair around her index finger. "No *way*. What happened?"

Ada's voice was overly relaxed, like she was trying desperately hard to seem chill. "She went skinny-dipping in the sea..." She paused for dramatic effect. "In the *middle* of the day! *So* cringe. I nearly died, like, literally."

Molly wanted to cry. Ada was *hugely* exaggerating, just to make the Populars like her. Molly's mom hadn't been taken to jail—just been given a little bit of a warning by a bossy police officer. She clenched her fist around her Tudors book.

"That's wild," Penalty Pete said. "My dad's in prison too."

"Wow!" Ada replied. "We have *so* much in common."

"Wait, your friend..." Felicity popped her bubble gum. "Is that one of the Seabrook sisters? They always smell like deep fryer grease in PE."

Molly froze, ice-cold hatred pulsing through her veins.

But it only got worse when Ada just giggled and said, "Yup."

# The Blowup

At the end of the day, Ada waited for Molly at the school gates, where they usually met to walk home together. Today, Molly simply barged past her, shoulders tensed huffily, and strode off in the direction of the lighthouse. The pace was very hard to maintain on account of her lack of physical fitness, but her stubbornness prevailed. She tried to disguise the panting as best she could yet still ended up sounding like a cocker spaniel who'd run a marathon.

Ada took off after her, jogging to keep up. "Mol? What's wrong?"

Molly struggled to keep the hurt out of her voice. "I heard you talking to Felicity Davison."

Ada fell silent for a moment, her cheeks tinged pink. "When?"

"You've spoken to her more than once?"

Chewing her bottom lip, Ada said defensively, "She's not as bad as you think, Mol."

"Well, she didn't seem to think much of my family."

"She was just *kidding*." Ada tilted her head to one side in a concerned way. "You always take everything so seriously."

Molly stopped in her tracks, swinging on her heel to face Ada. Anger bubbled in her belly, then started rising in her throat like vomit. "How could you gossip about my mom like that? You made us look even weirder than we already are."

Ada held up her palms in mock defense. "Chill out! It's just a funny story."

"To *you*, it's just a funny story, maybe, but to me, it's my *life*." Molly threw her backpack to the ground, and Ada jumped backward in shock. "How would you like it if I went around telling 'funny stories' about your parents getting divorced?"

"That's hardly the same—"

Molly put on a fake, giggly, popular-girl voice. "Hey, Felicity, did you hear about my friend's mom? She had an affair with a wrinkly seventy-year-old and left her family for him! Sooo funny, right?"

Ada's bottom lip quivered. "Stop, Mol—"

"Not very nice, is it?" Molly picked up her backpack and started walking again.

"*You're* not very nice," Ada shouted after her. "You're a horrible person. And you think you're so much better than Felicity Davison, but you're not."

"Fine! Go and share your barbecue potato chips with her, then!" This wasn't quite the searing insult Molly had intended, but she rolled with it. "Since she's so *great*." Much better.

"Maybe I will."

Ada stormed off in the other direction, back toward school, and Molly stalked the rest of the way home in furious silence. She hoped there was an oxygen tank waiting for her when she got through the door, because her lungs were about to explode from all the yelling and power walking.

However, she arrived back at Kittiwake Keep to find Minnie hurtling around the living room and kitchen in a figure eight. Her chocolate-stained face was frantic, her eyes wide, and she was chanting. "*Bad dog bad dog bad dog bad dog bad dog bad dog bad dog bad dog bad dog bad dog bad dog bad dog bad dog bad dog—*"

"She ate a box of seashell caramels," Mom explained, calmly looking at tax returns from the fish-and-chip shop.

Molly rolled her eyes. "For God's sake."

"*For dog's sake!*" Minnie skidded into a doorframe but looked completely unfazed, beginning her hurtling once again. "*I'm a bad dog bad dog bad dog—*"

Ditching her backpack by the table and beelining for the fridge, Molly said, "Shouldn't we get her stomach pumped or something?"

"Nah. She'll vomit it up soon enough."

Myla was also sitting at the kitchen table poring over some impossible-looking physics homework. She looked up. "Remember when Minnie had her appendix out, and when she woke up from the anesthesia, she looked down at her catheter and said, 'Goodbye, appendix. Hello, ding-dong'?"

Right at that moment, Minnie threw up all over the living-room floor. Unfortunately, she didn't stop running, so she sprinted straight into the waterfall of puke. Then she farted with the stress of it all.

Molly swore under her breath. Earnestly, Minnie glared at Molly and said, "Bad dog."

The stench of puke stung at Molly's nostrils, and she felt her temper rising once again. Breathing deeply, she attempted to control it as she peered into the fridge, willing some white chocolate to materialize.

The puke-soaked Minnie continued with her mad dash around the house, with neither Mom nor Myla making any attempt to stop her and give her a good hosing down.

Minnie tripped and stumbled over a chair leg and went crashing to the ground. Instead of wailing in pain, however, she just looked up with her big, round eyes and said, "That wasn't supposed to happen. Mommy, can I rip your eyelashes out?"

Mom frowned over the tax return, clearly unhappy at some of the numbers. "Maybe later, darling."

Minnie grinned manically. "I like eyelashes. They're delicious."

Slamming the fridge door shut, Molly felt herself lose the battle with her temper. It exploded from her mouth like Minnie's vomit.

"Arrrghhh! Why is this family so *weird*? Why can't we just be *normal*? Every other family in this *stupid* town is just... They're normal, but we're not, and I can't stand it! No *wonder* Ada's embarrassed to be friends with me. I wish..." She was about to say something awful, but Minnie's doleful red eyes forced the words back down. The lump in her throat bobbed like an ice cube. "Forget it."

Despite Molly's outburst, Myla didn't even bother looking up from her homework.

Mom just nodded, noncommittal. "Mmm, I know, yes. Can you go and shower Minnie?"

Strangely, washing her disgusting little sister was actually pretty therapeutic. The sugar high had worn off by the time Molly had stripped away Minnie's stinky clothes and pushed her into the shower. Minnie stood there motionless, like a particularly gross statue, while Molly rinsed her hair with lukewarm water and soft vanilla shampoo. Thankfully, showers didn't seem to produce enough water to cause a transformation, because Molly didn't think she had the energy to deal with a tail right now.

Molly was just fishing a chunk of boiled carrot out of Minnie's armpit when her little sister looked up at her, eyes gleaming, and said, "It was worth it."

Eventually, the water ran clear, so Molly gently toweled Minnie off and got her into the comfiest pajamas she could find. Throughout this process, Minnie only farted eight more times, which was actually a little on the light side.

Once Minnie was safely curled up by the fire, stroking her own hair and whispering, "Good dog," Molly retreated to her empty room. Melissa was out at a field hockey tournament, so Molly lay down on her bed with the lights still off and closed her eyes. Her blood thudded lightly in her ears—a hangover from the rage outburst.

Then, sure enough, the guilt began to grow.

This always happened after Molly lashed out at someone. At the time, it felt good and right, and she believed wholeheartedly in what she was saying. Immediately afterward, she was filled with triumphant self-righteousness. But eventually, once the adrenaline had worn off and she had time to think about what she'd done, invariably, she was filled with regret.

Had she overreacted about the Ada thing?

OK, so Ada had used Molly's mom's skinny-dipping as joke fodder, and yes, she'd just giggled and agreed when Felicity Davison was mean about Molly's fish-and-chip-shop smell. Plus, it was infuriating when Ada used that patronizing tone, which made Molly feel two inches tall.

Yet snapping back about Ada's parents' divorce was uncalled for. Ada had been devastated over the summer when it all came out, and Molly had just thrown that back in her face during a stupid argument.

How could she have done that?

Looking back, Molly knew she should've kept the moral high ground. She should have explained to Ada why she was hurt without stooping to insults.

Her eyes pricked with tears. She wished she wasn't like this. She lashed out so quickly and easily and then hated herself for it.

It felt so much better to be gentle and kind, like when she'd showered Minnie just now. So why couldn't she be like that all the time? It was like she wasn't in control of her own words and actions, much like the sea had no control over its tides.

The mood swings ruled her life, and she couldn't imagine that changing anytime soon.

## CHAPTER

## 9

·····················

# What's Your Trout?

ater that evening, Molly had finished a very slow
shift at the shop and was changing into her jammies
when Melissa and Margot barged into the bedroom. Molly
yelped and attempted to cover herself with a Seabrook's
menu, which was nowhere near extensive enough to shield
her newly blossoming chest. Her sisters didn't even have the
common decency to look embarrassed.

"Dude, what's your trout?" Margot asked.

The Seabrook sisters had always said this instead of
"what's your beef?" because it was important to promote
brand awareness at every opportunity.

"What?" Molly said, utterly fed up at this point.

"You're stomping around like you're in a very angry
music video."

Molly sighed. "Me and Ada had a falling-out."

"What? How come?" Melissa said, blinking as her bangs flopped into her eyes.

Molly hastily filled them in on the drama, followed by the awful things she had said. "I feel pretty bad about it."

"Why?" Margot shrugged. "Sounds like Ada was a patronizing turd."

"How exactly would a turd be patronizing?" asked Molly.

"Listening to you two talk is like watching chimpanzees argue about bananas," Melissa interjected. "Molly, you *really* shouldn't get angry at people like that. It's going to get you in *serious* trouble one day, you know. What if it was a teacher you lost your temper with?"

"You know it's not illegal to get angry, right, Melissa?" Margot said.

"Still, it's *not* very smart to mouth off to a teacher, is it?"

Molly rolled her eyes. "Yes, well, thankfully, Ada is thirteen and therefore not a math professor."

"*Anyway*," Margot said, shooting a bored look at Melissa and flopping on to the bed covered in stuffed penguins. "We're playing mermaids tonight. In the actual sea and everything. And you're coming with us."

Molly started to protest. "But I—"

"I cannot emphasize enough how little I care about your excuses. You're coming. End of story. *Finito*."

Turning her back and quickly tugging a grubby oversized T-shirt over her head, Molly muttered, "I don't want to. End of story. *Finito*. And besides, didn't Mom say we shouldn't go in the deep sea? Isn't it dangerous or something? Because of the poop?"

"Only the really deep parts," Margot said, twiddling the tassel on Molly's bedspread. "I've been in lots of times and I'm absolutely fine. No damage done."

"Debatable," Molly retorted, then turned to Melissa. "Hey, how come you're so up for this? Going against Mom's word and all."

Melissa chewed her lip as though she was worried about this deep down. "I don't think it's as dangerous as she says it is. We don't go *that* far. And I like spending time as a mermaid. With...you guys." She flushed bright red as she said this, as if admitting to liking her sisters' company was a source of great embarrassment.

Molly shoved her feet into her slippers. "Still no."

"Why not?" Margot pouted, which did not suit her in the slightest.

"Because I don't want to be a *freak*. I just want to be normal, OK?"

Margot scoffed and rolled her eyes. "And *popular*."

Cheeks burning, Molly fought the urge to stamp her foot. "That's not true."

"Ridiculous. You think we don't notice when you spend your entire lunch break staring at Steve Cox and the giggling girls who follow him around like ducklings chasing their mother? We have to clean up your drool with a mop."

Molly hated how obvious she was, and she hated Margot for making her feel even worse about it. With an air of finality, she said, "I'm not coming."

"Please, Molly," Melissa pleaded. "It's an important day for Margot."

"Why?" Molly muttered. "Is she marrying a squid? Starting her first day of work over in Loony Town?"

"She has a derby match."

"*The* derby match." Margot had a smug look on her face.

"What?"

"Marmouth Marlins versus Tweedtown Trevallies."

Molly rolled her eyes. "Oh, when you say it like that, it makes total sense."

"Clamdunk," Margot said simply.

Melissa nodded enthusiastically. "The mermaid sport."

Molly scoffed. "I suppose the sea's too wet for soccer."

"Margot's the youngest player ever to make it to the premier league."

Molly shook her head. "Obviously. Does Mom know about this?"

"God, you sound like Melissa," Margot muttered. Melissa shot her a death stare. "No, she doesn't know. So keep your lips sealed, all right? Snitches get stitches."

"Are we gangsters now?" Molly asked, wondering vaguely what a gang of mermaids might look like.

"Please come, Molly." Melissa wrung her hands. "Margot's nervous."

Margot glared, clearly offended. "Am not."

"She wants you there."

"Do not."

But Melissa was right, Molly thought. Margot *did* look nervous. She clenched her fists tightly as though to stop her fingers from trembling, and her face was pale and clammy.

"Fine, but I don't want to risk anyone seeing us," Molly mumbled. "Even when it's dark, you can still see down to the beach from the boardwalk." This, at least, was the truth.

"First, cute that you think this takes place on the beach, like volleyball or some other basic human sport." Margot folded her arms. "Second, cute that you don't think I have at least half a dozen secret ways out of this lighthouse."

Molly must've still looked unconvinced, because then Margot smiled gently, which Molly did not think she was capable of doing. Her usual expression was a troublemaking smirk.

"Look, Mol. This happens. It does. Your body *wants* to be a mermaid. It's what feels most natural to it. So when you deprive your body of its natural state for too long, the frustration starts to build up inside you. Eventually, it bubbles over. We've all learned that lesson the hard way." A pointed look at Melissa. "*All* of us."

Could this be true? Could her angry outbursts really not be entirely her fault?

"But I've been like this for years," Molly whispered. "It can't just be the mermaid thing. Can it?"

"No," Margot admitted. "You are also a grumpy goat. But the mermaid thing doesn't help. I promise you'll feel more calm and level once you've spent some time in the sea."

Molly wanted so badly for this to be true. All right, so it wouldn't make what happened with Ada any better. The damage was already done. But if there was something she could do to prevent it from happening again, it had to be worth a try.

She took a deep breath. "OK. I believe you. Which is probably a mistake, because last time I believed you, I ate a dead housefly thinking it was a raisin."

Margot beamed. "Good times."

# The Trapdoor

*W*hen it came to hidden passageways out of the lighthouse, Margot was as good as her word.

Once Mom had gone to bed, Molly, Margot, and Melissa snuck down the creaky spiral staircase and slipped through the living room into the semicircular kitchen. Margot made a beeline to the broken dishwasher and promptly began tugging it away from the wall.

"I'm not sure a broken dishwasher is going to make us transform," Molly whispered.

"Oh, please shut up for once in your life," Margot muttered, huffing and puffing as she finally hoisted the dishwasher into the center of the room. Molly remembered what she'd said about how her superhuman strength was only accessible when she was a mermaid. If she had a tail right now, she'd probably be able to perform a conga with the dishwasher, the oven, and the kitchen table.

To Molly's astonishment, there was a trapdoor beneath the spot where the broken dishwasher had always sat. Working as silently as possible, Margot opened the trapdoor to reveal an old rope ladder leading down to...somewhere.

Molly's chest pounded with excitement. As a kid living in an abandoned lighthouse, this was the kind of thing she'd always dreamed about. Trick stairs, hidden treasure, ghosts and ghouls haunting the creepy attic, pulling a book off a bookcase shelf to watch the whole thing swing open and reveal dusty old rooms nobody knew about but her.

And now there was a trapdoor in the kitchen! Molly could hardly contain her squeals of anticipation. Margot descended first, followed by Melissa. Molly practically flew down after them, nearly sliding her foot off one rung. She was so desperate to see what was in this secret cellar that she couldn't control her haste.

At first, Molly was a little disappointed. The circular room was lit by small lights studded around the walls, but as her eyes adjusted to the dimness, all she could make out were bookshelves. Lots and lots of bookshelves, each and every one full to bursting with old leather-bound books.

Reading Molly's expression, Margot said, "Take a closer look."

Running her index finger over the nearest antique volume, Molly peered at its title: *Aquata: A Complete Biography of Meire's Iconic Founder.* A look along the rest of the row revealed more mermish books: *Mythical Merfolk and their Astounding Ancestry, A Beginner's Guide to Subaquatic Astrology, A Short History of the Great Meire-Syreni War.* Dozens upon dozens of books dedicated to her very own heritage. Were these the ancient aquatic texts Myla studied with her merpower?

To Molly's surprise, her heart tugged toward them, begging her to open one. She wasn't really a book person, but there was something about the mysterious, dusty volumes that seemed forbidden and exciting.

Molly was so absorbed in the books and their romantic smell that she'd barely noticed Margot, who was grunting and turning a heavy lever in the wooden floorboards. Molly gasped. The floorboards were opening, a gigantic circular hole revealing itself in the ground. Below them was the sea itself, whirling and splashing and roaring like a beast come to life.

"Is that...?" Melissa whispered, awestruck, her buttercup-yellow tail materializing seamlessly.

Molly's legs prickled. Her joints began to ache and twist,

and with the sensations came a sense of dread. As her shiny white tail completed its transformation, she could barely look at it. Why did it have to be so *boring*?

"Does Mom know about this?" Molly asked, staring into the watery maelstrom below. Her white top appeared magically. Seafoam sprayed her from head to tail, and she shivered.

"Why do you think she bought an abandoned lighthouse in the first place?" Margot said.

"I just thought she was a little weird."

"Well, that too. But Mom doesn't know *I* know, so keep quiet, OK?"

"Yeah!" Molly said, at the exact same time as Melissa said, "How can you *possibly* expect us to keep yet another one of your secrets, Margot?"

"All right, on three," Margot announced. "One...two..."

"Wait! What are we doing on three?" Molly asked.

"The macarena," replied Margot.

Melissa rolled her eyes. "We're jumping, I assume."

"Forgot about your inbuilt lie detector," Margot muttered.

Molly's heart skipped. Her first swim as a mermaid...

"OK, for real this time. One...two..."

But Margot never got to three. Instead, she shoved both Molly and Melissa over the side with her superhuman strength, cackling gleefully as she did so.

The bottom dropped out of Molly's stomach, and she plunged into the water. The world went quiet.

Usually, whenever Molly went in the sea, she loathed every second. The salt stung her eyes, cracked her lips, turned her stomach. The bitter cold numbed her skin and ached in her bones. The swelling undercurrent filled her with panic until she was certain she'd be dragged below the surface, get tangled in a clump of seaweed, and be savaged to death by a school of cod seeking revenge for the many family members they'd lost to the Seabrook fish-and-chip shop.

Of course, that was before she had a tail.

Molly quickly discovered that when you're a mermaid, it's different. Very different. The salt felt fresh and invigorating. The cold was no longer cold; in fact, the temperature perfectly matched her own, so it didn't feel like she was submerged in water at all. The currents thrummed with energy and life. And she could *breathe*. The feeling in her lungs was so crisp and cool, it was like standing on a mountaintop and taking in huge gulps of pure air.

Her other senses were heightened too. She could hear Melissa arguing viciously about Margot pushing them in early. She could see far into the depths of the sea, picking out eels and clusters of coral.

And fish. So many fish.

(Not quite as many as a traditional Seabrook birthday party, but still.)

"Right, this way!" Margot said, then started swimming in a sharp downward direction.

Molly raised an eyebrow at Melissa, who said, "She's telling the truth for once."

They swam behind Margot until they reached what looked like an underwater cliff. The wall of rock had a small diamond-shaped opening, which Margot squeezed through until she disappeared into whatever was on the other side. Melissa and Molly followed.

They continued into another body of water, but it was warmer now. Then, to Molly's surprise, they began propelling themselves directly upward until they broke through the surface.

"Welcome to Coley Cavern!" Margot announced proudly.

Molly gasped. They were in some kind of huge cave with the sea filling its middle. The water glimmered beneath a string of lanterns hanging from the cavern's ceiling. The rocks glistened with sea spray, and waves lapped gently against the rugged walls.

And perhaps most notably of all, Coley Cavern was full of merfolk.

Molly rubbed her eyes, but this was no dream. Elegant

mermaids perched effortlessly on the slippery rocks, their rainbow array of tails shining in the twinkling lights, while mermen—with pointy little horns on the sides of their heads—splashed in pools with their merchildren, teaching them a complex-looking game with a pearl-like ball. It was strange to Molly that these kids had grown up knowing who—or what—they were.

Clutching a giant spear, an ancient merman with a beard as long as his tail snoozed on the shore, the tide lapping at his ankles. Or, you know, the place where his ankles should've been if he wasn't an *ancient merman clutching a giant spear.*

"Old Alan," Margot said triumphantly.

"This seems fine," Molly replied. "Absolutely normal. Boring, if anything."

## CHAPTER

# 11

......................

# *Clamdunk*

The echoing of the cavern rang in Molly's ears. She was so overwhelmed by the sight of the merfolk in front of her that she almost forgot why they were here: to watch Margot play clamdunk. Whatever that was.

The oval of water inside the cove had been cordoned off with ropes of seashells, and two huge clam-like goals had been set up at either end. Looking increasingly pale, Margot waved goodbye to her sisters and swam away to a small cave tucked away at the north end of the cavern. Haphazardly pinned above the entrance was a driftwood sign reading "HOME TEAM."

Melissa and Molly swam around trying to find a good spot to watch the game from and found an ideal perch on the half-moon crescent of jutting rocks overlooking the sea field.

As they sat down and tried to catch their breath, Molly found that it was a strange sensation being above water once again. It wasn't quite as easy to breathe as it was while submerged, and a twinging in her chest told her she was craving another dive in. Maybe this was what Margot had meant about her "natural state."

Although Molly had no real problem talking to strangers—a perk of spending half her life dressed as a haddock and cramming flyers into touristy hands—she found herself being very content to sit and watch the other mermaids go about their lives. She smiled as she watched two teenage mermaids gossiping behind a rock, like she and Ada did in the locker nook.

The thought sent another pang of guilt cutting through her chest. She forced Ada from her mind.

What was this mysterious mermaid sport going to be like? And how did Margot become good enough to play for a real team, even though she grew up on dry land?

Molly really, really hoped Margot played well. She was always so grumpy when she lost at anything. Once, her team had lost a badminton tournament in the first round, and she'd put a "For Sale" sign outside the lighthouse. Apparently, she couldn't possibly stay in Little Marmouth after such a crushing defeat.

Right at that moment, two dozen players in opposing green and burgundy jerseys swam on to the field faster than Molly even believed possible.

The crowd cheered them as they swam around, each holding what looked like a fishing net. The ball looked like a giant pearl, and they threw it to each other's nets while advancing up the sea field toward the clam-shaped goal. From what Molly could tell, the sport was halfway between water polo and lacrosse.

Molly's stomach gave a funny lurch as she watched Margot begin the warm-up with her teammates. She kept trying to catch a ball in a net and missed every time.

Molly'd always felt the churning shame in her own belly whenever one of her sisters did something embarrassing. Secondhand humiliation between Seabrooks was strong, and she could feel Margot's mortification as strongly as if it were her own.

Before long, the game started. Margot was one of the first to gain possession of the ball, but her attempt at a pass was quickly intercepted by the opposition, and her teammate gestured furiously at her. Molly cringed as the Tweedtown Trevallies landed the pearl in the back of the Marlins' goal, and the keeper—an angry-looking mermaid with cropped pink hair—kicked the stick of her net in frustration.

It all seemed simple enough to grasp...until the first snatch.

At first, Molly couldn't tell what was happening. All she saw was a burgundy blur as a burly Trevally launched herself at an opponent swimming a few yards in front of her. She reached out and grabbed something that had been nesting in the crook of the Marlin's tail—another tiny pearl. The second it was removed, the Marlin froze, unable to move, and a loud horn blared.

A rapturous cheer erupted through the cavern as the player was removed from the field by two referees with striped tails.

Molly turned to her sister, who was watching intently. "Melissa. I have questions."

"Right! Yes. Sorry. Want a quick lesson on the rules?"

Molly nodded gratefully.

"Twelve players per team: one keeper, nine chalkers, and two hawkers. The chalkers focus on scoring goals, while the hawkers scoot around stealing pearlilles—the tiny tail pearls—from their opponents. Once a pearlille is gone, it's gone for the whole game, and the player has to leave the field."

Molly watched as another Marlin was frozen and escorted away.

"The game only ends once every chalker on a team has lost their pearlille. So it's ten points for every clamdunk—that's what it's called when you score a goal—and minus ten points for every player who loses their pearlille. Winner is the team with the highest score once the game is over, which is *usually* always the team with their pearlilles still intact. There have been some upsets, though. In last year's semifinal, the Narwhals lost by 940 points to 980, even though their opponents had all lost their pearlilles. The hawker was so exhausted, she didn't realize her team were behind, and she stole the last pearlille without realizing it'd lose them the match." Melissa shook her head in dismay. "What an *idiot.*"

In the time Melissa had been talking, no fewer than four Marlin chalkers had lost their pearlilles. The game was now spectacularly one-sided, and the Trevallies were winning 140–0. Margot was still on the field but barely. Molly watched as the opposition repeatedly lunged at her sister, narrowly missing her pearlille.

Then something truly amazing happened. A Marlin chalker tossed the ball to Margot, who made a spectacular crashing dive in order to catch it. She arced out of the water with gushing speed and almost threw her arm out of its socket to scoop the ball out of the air and into her net.

The crowd cheered. This success seemed to spur Margot on. Fixing a look of determination on her face, she set off up the field.

Weaving through Trevallies, seaweed clumps, and enormous rock clusters, Margot moved at ultraspeed. She evaded capture no fewer than five times, then hurled the ball into the back of the goal.

Molly and Melissa screamed, fist pumping and whooping as though Margot had just won an Olympic gold medal.

But instead of celebrating, Margot darted back to the middle of the field, ready to go again. Once play resumed, she intercepted a pass between Trevallies and did the exact same frantic dash up toward the goal.

Molly couldn't make sense of how fast her sister was moving. It was like she was a speedboat, and everyone else on the field was a goldfish.

She scored again. The crowd went wild.

"How is she so good at this?" Molly asked Melissa reverently.

"The merpower," Melissa whispered. "Her strength helps her propel through the water at lightning speed—and makes her throws so powerful, the keeper has no chance of stopping them. Some of the others have athletic merpowers too, but none of them are as strong as Margot."

The same thing kept happening, with Margot moving far too quickly for anyone else to catch her. She put ball after ball in the back of the net, even as the rest of her teammates lost their pearlilles. Even when she was the only chalker left on the field for the Marlins, she swam rings around her opponents until the scoreboard was tied at 140–140.

One Trevally was so angry that she snapped her net in half before being confronted with what looked like the clamdunk version of a penalty card—a shell painted daffodil yellow. Margot barely noticed.

Again and again, she scored, until she was easily a hundred points ahead. Her teammates watched in astonishment as their humiliating defeat turned into a stunning victory.

Eventually, a hawker managed to grip the very end of Margot's tail and remove her pearlille, ending the game even though it meant they lost. They were obviously sick of being humiliated, and there was no chance of catching up with the Marlins now.

"We won!" Melissa yelled.

Margot finally let herself smile and looked around at the adoring crowd as though only just noticing they were there. Her teammates swarmed around her, lifting her up onto their shoulders and chanting some kind of victory song, which echoed so dramatically around the cavern that Molly was sure their mom would hear it up in the lighthouse.

Watching Margot celebrate, Molly's heart swelled with pride. That was the thing about sisters: sure, you inherited their shame and embarrassment, but when they did something truly *amazing*, their happiness was your very own.

# Back to Reality

O nce the high of the clamdunk victory had finally worn off—Margot stayed up chattering excitedly in Melissa and Molly's room until the sun came up—the reality of the school day ahead sunk in. Not only did Molly have to deal with the aftermath of her ugly fight with Ada, but she had to do it on about forty minutes of sleep.

Oh, and she'd forgotten to do her math homework. Somehow, she didn't think "a walrus ate my quadratic equations" was going to fly with Ms. Stavros.

It was English first, which Molly didn't share with Ada, so she had some time to brainstorm ideas on how to make up with her best friend while pretending to be listening to Mrs. Wilson drone on about the Romantic poets.

*How romantic could they be if they didn't write about onion rings or tubas?*

Molly chuckled to herself at the joke and promptly wrote it down to tell Ada once they were friends again. Now that the heat of the moment was long gone, Molly couldn't understand what she'd been so upset about yesterday. It had all been blown way out of proportion, and she would be more than happy to apologize, as long as Ada agreed to talk to her.

*Wow, did I just have a mature thought?* Molly was deeply shocked at herself. The only mature thought she'd previously had in her life was about which cheddar cheese to buy from the grocery store.

Maybe Margot was right. She *did* feel more calm and centered after her jaunt to Coley Cavern. Could it be that spending time as a mermaid really was crucial to her happiness?

Molly shuddered. Hopefully not. She wanted to be normal, not spend her time watching fantastic creatures romping around an underwater cavern throwing pearls at each other.

The second the bell rang for morning recess, Molly practically sprinted out of the classroom to find Ada. Well, not *sprinted* exactly. If Molly tried to sprint, she was sure her legs would crumple like a Coke can from the shock of it all.

However, when she got to Ada's locker, she was dismayed to find her best friend standing there with Felicity Davison. Felicity Davison with her stupid long legs and stupid blond hair and stupid...*face*.

Maybe the rage hadn't disappeared entirely.

As Molly rummaged in her own locker, she kept trying to meet Ada's eye, but Ada was pointedly ignoring her. Ada's tie was significantly shorter than yesterday. Plus, Molly couldn't help but notice that both Felicity and Ada had rolled up their skirts so far that there was more roll than skirt. It looked like they had added tires around their waists. Molly couldn't remember ever seeing this look on Ariana Grande, but maybe it would catch on soon enough.

Felicity was half texting, half babbling at Ada. "You're just, like, way cooler than the girls in my grade. I don't normally get along with other girls, but you're fun. I can see why Pete likes you."

"He does?" Ada grinned, checking her lip gloss in a pop-up mirror that definitely hadn't been in her locker last week.

"Duh. Want to go watch them play?"

And then they were off, and Molly had lost her chance to make amends.

Slamming her locker shut with a clang, Molly sighed. Would Ada even *want* to be friends with her again? Now that she was in with the popular group, she had no need for a dweeby best friend who smelled like battered haddock.

In geography, when she'd usually sit next to Ada, Molly decided to postpone the drama and instead opted for the seat next to Eddie of the Ears.

"Hey." She smiled at him, but he barely looked up. He was jotting something furiously in his notebook.

"Haven't seen you at the chip shop lately," she said, unpacking her books. "We're overflowing with uneaten fried pieces."

Eddie grinned but again didn't look up. "Yeah. I've been—"

"Just when you're all ready!" Mr. Li barked before opening up his presentation on river formations.

Because Eddie of the Ears wasn't allowed to wear his beanie in school, his crown of flaming-red hair was flying out of control. It was practically a supernova, Molly thought, if supernovas smelled like AXE body spray. He kept running his hand through it self-consciously as he took notes, tugging at the ends as though urging them to cover his lobes.

Molly was surprised how eager a student Eddie was. She had always thought of him as the class clown because he was so funny, but he actually paid close attention to everything Mr. Li was saying.

Right then, inspiration struck, and Molly came up with probably the funniest geography joke she'd ever thought of.

Without Ada to share it with, she hastily scribbled it on a scrap of paper and handed it to Eddie of the Ears.

*Why do sharks only swim in saltwater?*

He shrugged with a half smile. She scribbled furiously.

*Because pepper makes them sneeze.*

A smile quirked at the corners of Eddie's lips, but he turned his attention back to the whiteboard, and his gaze remained there for the rest of the class. When the bell rang, he stayed behind to ask Mr. Li something. Who knew the class clown was such a brainiac?

Finally, it was lunch. Spotting Margot sitting alone in the cafeteria, Molly plonked herself down and sighed emphatically. "This day is garbage."

Margot's dark eyes were twinkling like they always were when she was up to mischief. "It's about to get a whole lot better. Watch."

Margot gestured to the popular table, where Ada was about to chomp into her ketchup-slathered hot dog. She'd obviously switched from packed lunches so she could spend more time with Felicity and Penalty Pete. As she bit off a giant hunk, her face immediately flushed red and sweaty, and she coughed and spluttered and gasped.

"What did you do?" Molly muttered under her breath at a snickering Margot.

"Cayenne pepper in the ketchup."

"Margot!"

"What?" Tears of laughter were streaming down her freckled face, taking her black-winged eyeliner with them. "I don't like how snotty she was about the shop, all right?" She wiped her tears on Molly's tie. "And I remembered how much she hates spicy stuff. Relax! It's funny."

Frowning and adjusting her tie, Molly wasn't sure if it *was* funny. Though admittedly, watching Ada desperately swig from a carton of pineapple juice, shiny bangs stuck to her forehead with sweat, was rather satisfying. Especially since Felicity looked completely grossed out by the whole thing.

But Molly didn't want to sabotage her chances at making up with Ada, and besides, they had both been in the wrong.

After lunch, Molly's class was forced to endure forty minutes of field hockey on a cold, wet field. Although briefly concerned that the pouring rain might cause her to switch to schmermaid status, Molly's fears turned out to be unfounded, and she managed to waste over half of the match applying new tape to her beaten-up hockey stick. This was a regular tactic of hers, and there were currently at least seven layers of tape up on the handle. Only a person with hands the size of oars could use it.

Weak from lack of sleep, Molly found herself hanging around in the locker room long after everyone else had gone to afternoon recess, trying to tame her frizzy mane.

Spotting a hair straightener someone had left plugged in by the chipped mirror, an idea struck her. Maybe if she could make herself look more glamorous, like Ada, then she'd stand a chance at making it with the Populars too. It had to be worth a shot.

Fifteen minutes later, she'd just managed to wrangle her hair into something resembling a sleek ponytail when Ada stalked into the locker room. She looked straight at the mirror, to where Molly stood adjusting her hair tie. Molly's heart leaped, but it was fleeting.

"Why are you using my straightener?" Ada snapped, sniffing the air. "Oh, gross. You've made it stink like deep fryer grease."

Molly stared at the ground. "Sorry."

Ada wrinkled her nose. "Might as well keep it. There's no *way* I'm using it now."

Normally, Molly would hurl an equally mean insult back at Ada, but today, she was simply too tired, and Ada's words stung. Her eyes filled with tears, and she sprinted from the locker room as fast as she could.

Right into a giant puddle that had formed outside.

The tingling started almost instantly. In a fit of panic, Molly tore off her coat and threw it over her legs just in time. Crying out involuntarily, she hit the ground hard as her tail flopped to life.

Ada burst through the door. "I'm sorry, Mol—oh my God, Molly! Are you OK?"

"Flaganshmood," said Molly through a mouthful of muddy puddle water.

Ada dumped her backpack on the wet tarmac and crouched down beside Molly. "Are you hurt? Here, let me help you up." She held out a hand, concern etched all over her face.

As badly as Molly wanted to accept Ada's olive branch, she couldn't. What was it Melissa had said? About keeping her mermaidness a secret? *"We can't talk about that at school. Not ever, do you understand me? We could get in so much trouble!"*

Even Margot had seemed frightened about what could happen if they accidentally let word get out.

Panic building in her chest, Molly pulled back as though Ada's palm was carrying a fatal contagious disease. "No! Get away from me!"

Ada's face crumpled. "I'm so sorry, Mol. I shouldn't have said—"

Molly's eyes filled with fresh tears. Pushing away her old

best friend was as painful as the bruise blooming on her hip. She readjusted the coat to make sure it was fully covering her tail.

"Please. Go away. Please."

Ada did, and Molly felt thoroughly miserable as she leopard-crawled away from the puddle and returned to the Land of the Footed.

By the time her evening shift rolled around, Molly's eyes were stinging with exhaustion. Three bleak hours of handing out leaflets in lashing rain lay ahead of her, on a night when nobody in their right mind was out on the boardwalk.

Molly yawned once again, fantasizing about how good it would be to have a hot bath and curl up in her rickety bed with a cup of hot chocolate. When she got home, she'd even ask Minnie to climb in with her, and they could read some chapters of her latest library book together. All right, so it might be kind of a squeeze if Minnie insisted on wearing her clompy jelly shoes and brought along her full menagerie of stuffed animals. But it would be cozy to say the least.

However, as so often happens with siblings, that night, Minnie decided to be annoying instead of cute. Sopping wet and shivering, Molly arrived back at Kittiwake Keep to find her mom towel-drying Minnie's long dark hair by the fireplace. Melissa and Margot were still closing up at the shop, while Myla was studying upstairs despite the fact that her final exams weren't until June.

"Where was you last night?" Minnie accused Molly the second she walked in.

Molly froze. Mom had no idea the sisters had gone to a clamdunk game. They weren't supposed to be in the sea at all. And as airy-fairy as their mom was, she would probably lose it at the thought of her daughters putting themselves in danger just for a pointless sport like clamdunk.

"What are you talking about, silly?" Molly said, trying to play it cool. "I was in bed."

"You wasn't." Minnie shook her head violently, ruining the French braid Mom was attempting. "I had a nightmare an' I came looking. You wasn't there. None of you was."

"Were," Mom corrected half-heartedly. She looked as exhausted as Molly felt. Her chest looked particularly bony, and the sight made Molly's stomach twinge. It reminded her of the horrible days while Mom was enduring chemo and could barely get out of bed, let alone eat.

Molly slumped down into the oldest, squashiest armchair. The heat of the fire was delicious on her wet face. "Maybe that was part of your nightmare, scampi. Have you been eating cheese before bed again?"

Frowning, Minnie mumbled, "Momma, they wasn't there. I swear they wasn't."

"The boardwalk was dead tonight," Molly interrupted, changing the subject to avoid this line of questioning. She didn't want to get Margot in trouble, as much as Margot often deserved it. "Hardly anyone out."

"How can a boardwalk die?" Minnie asked sincerely, picking at a piece of dry skin on her thumb. "Did it have an-an-an-aneurysm?"

"It's a figure of... Never mind."

Looking worried, Minnie said, "We wouldn't be able to bury the boardwalk. It's too big. We'd have to burn it like Granny."

It wasn't funny, but it made Molly laugh anyway. It had been a long day.

"Come on, toots." Arms heavy with fatigue, Mom tied up the braid as best she could and patted Minnie on the rear. "Time for bed."

Minnie did not take the news well. "Nooo!" she screamed at fever pitch. "I don't want to! Please, Mommaaa! Nooo!"

With her little sister shrill and hysterical, Molly felt the last of her patience wane. Kicking her soggy shoes into the corner of the room, she said to her mom, "I'm off for a bath."

"There's no hot water. Minnie used it all. You'll have to wait."

"OK. I'll fill the kettle. Maybe boil Minnie's head while I'm at it."

For some reason, this only made Minnie cry harder.

CHAPTER

# 13

......................

# Jack-in-the-Box

By the time a new week rolled around, Molly and Ada still hadn't made up. Every time Molly caught sight of her in the hallway, she was tagging along behind Felicity Davison or ogling Penalty Pete as he licked his shin pads (or whatever soccer fanatics actually did to pass the time).

Somehow, Ada was arriving early to all the classes she shared with Molly and making sure she nabbed a seat by the popular guys in their own grade. The likes of Conan and his cronies were starting to pay more attention to her now that she hung out with Penalty Pete, and Ada was loving every second of it. It was as if they thought she held the key to Pete's soccer skills.

One afternoon in history, Molly managed to grab a seat next to Ada, but as soon as class started, Ada told Mr.

Hackney that she'd forgotten her glasses and couldn't see the board. Someone up front switched with her. Miraculously, by the following day, when Molly sat away from her, Ada's eyesight was back to eagle levels. The laser-eye-surgery fairy must have paid her a visit in the night.

To make matters even worse, there were rumors that Cute Steve was now going out with Felicity Davison.

Molly knew it was stupid to be upset, since she never really had a chance with him anyway, but she couldn't help but feel disappointed. She had been foolish to imagine he might have chosen her over someone perfect and popular like Felicity, but it still felt like someone was clamping her heart in a tight fist whenever she thought about it. Maybe it felt so much worse because she didn't have Ada to mope with.

As usual, Molly's sadness was spilling out into anger— mainly toward Felicity. How could Cute Steve have such terrible taste? Yes, Felicity was pretty and charming, but she was so mean about Molly's family. Plus, she had already had lip fillers, even though she was only fourteen. Her eager-to-please stepdad knew a sketchy guy who didn't ask for ID apparently. She looked like she'd gone mouth-first into a beehive during honey season.

The dating rumors were confirmed one rainy after-noon recess, when Molly walked in on Cute Steve and Felicity tongue-kissing behind the stage in the theater. Molly had only ever been kissed by Minnie (who had drooled all over Molly's cheeks) and so expected to feel jealous, but she strangely didn't. It looked very wet and unpleasant.

She did wonder how Cute Steve could be having a good time, when surely lip fillers were very firm and uncomfortable. It must be like kissing a kitchen table.

In all fairness, he did look relieved by the distraction and smiled awkwardly at Molly as she deposited the props back in the costume trunk. However, before Molly had even left, Felicity was back to clamping her wooden lips around his. It looked like a lamb feeding from a bottle.

As upset as Molly was about the love of her life having his face sucked by another girl, she made herself feel better with the thought that she was well overdue for a blossoming. She'd witnessed the phenomenon when people randomly got really attractive over the space of one long holiday weekend. That was certainly going to happen to her soon. It was just a matter of time. Until then, she would simply focus on her razor-sharp wit and insight.

"Goodbye, table sucker," she said as she left the theater.

On second thought, maybe that wasn't the hilarious joke she thought it was. Thankfully, neither of them seemed to hear her.

Or maybe it was just that Cute Steve's sense of humor was broken. At lunchtime the next day, Margot's eyes had the prank glisten, and Molly's stomach sank. Was she targeting Ada yet again? But her troublesome sister had other ideas.

"Listen," Margot whispered, casting a glance over at the popular table. Cute Steve and Penalty Pete were mid-rant about some sort of upcoming soccer match. Ada and Felicity sat in stilted silence, picking at their lasagna and staring at their phones. Felicity's other friends, Jenna and Briony, were nowhere to be seen.

Margot pulled one half of Minnie's old baby monitor out of her pocket, pressed the microphone button, and started making a gurgly groaning noise into it, like a monster giving birth.

When Molly looked back to the popular table, Cute Steve had stopped talking about some team's new manager and was sitting stock-still, ears pricked up. He swung his head wildly from side to side, trying to find the source of the noise.

Margot smirked and gestured to the monitor in her palm. "The other half's stashed in his backpack. I've been bugging him with it all morning. His German teacher wasn't overly impressed." She frowned in a German sort of manner. "*Nicht gut, Herr Cox!*"

At the end of lunch, Margot found the baby monitor

dumped at the top of the cafeteria trash can. Molly found herself feeling a little disappointed. It would've been far funnier for Cute Steve to start messing with Margot in return, but he'd just thrown it away and continued to press his mouth against his wooden girlfriend.

After suffering through biology, Molly traipsed down to the locker room to get ready for field hockey. *Again.* Why were schools so obsessed with thwacking balls with wooden sticks? She hoped she'd be put in as goalie this time so she could have a quick nap behind her helmet without anyone noticing.

The athletic center was a quarter of a mile away from the main school building, tucked down a wooded sidewalk. Dragging her limp plastic bag of hand-me-down gym equipment behind her, Molly was in a world of her own, fantasizing about waxing off Felicity's eyebrows.

"Uh, hey…" came a gravelly voice beside her.

With a jolt, Molly looked up. Cute Steve, already in his gym shorts and blue polo shirt, scratched awkwardly at a scab on his elbow.

"All right?" he asked gruffly.

Molly looked behind her. Surely, the most popular guy in school wasn't talking to her? Voluntarily? Of his own free will? With no onion rings involved whatsoever?

"Uh, yes. Why?" In her shock and amazement, Molly

realized she sounded a little rude. "I mean, yeah, I'm good, thanks. How are you?"

"I'm good." Cute Steve ran a hand through his hair, and Molly dragged her gaze away so she didn't look like a lovestruck freak.

Seriously, how was this happening? Had Cute Steve been robbed and he needed her assistance in calling the police? Had they both stumbled into some kind of alternate reality where extremely cool and attractive ninth grade boys willingly spent time with awkward seventh grade girls who also happened to be mermaids?

Oh God. He was here about the baby monitor, wasn't he? She was supposed to make Cute Steve think she was mature and cool, not a childish prankster!

*Thanks, Margot.*

After a strangely long pause, Cute Steve said slowly, "So... your friend, Ada. Er, yeah."

Molly nodded, keeping very cool and nonchalant, trying to copy Cute Steve's relaxed manner. "Er, yeah. What about her?"

"Penalty wants to ask her out."

Great. Molly fought back the scowl. "Good for Penalty. I hope he scores." She was very pleased with this pun, but Cute Steve didn't seem to notice her comic genius.

Cute Steve rubbed the back of his neck. "You think you could ask her out for him?"

Molly laughed, suddenly feeling like she was in elementary school again. "Are you kidding?"

Cute Steve kicked a stone as they walked. It skittered to the foot of a nearby tree. "Well, s'awkward, isn't it? Asking people out."

"I guess so," Molly muttered, drawing on her vast experience of asking zero people out.

She had meant she guessed it was awkward, but Cute Steve took it to mean she guessed she'd do it. "Thanks," he said. "You're the best."

Molly smiled, her veins tingling pleasantly at the validation. She racked her brain for ways to keep the conversation running.

*Quick,* she thought, *think of something hilarious!*

However, Molly had no idea what sort of thing ninth graders found funny. Boobs? Farts? Bananas?

In the end, she just made a weird, wet, lip-smacking noise as she tried to swallow the excess saliva forming in her mouth.

"Anyway." Cute Steve waved to his friends up ahead, then turned to face her again. His deep brown eyes were warm and soft.

The tingling in Molly's veins intensified, beginning in the tips of her toes and spreading north—

*Oh. Oh, no.*

The swimming pool. Molly had been so busy focusing on Cute Steve that she hadn't noticed how close they were to the building. Usually, she looped around the long way to the athletic center to avoid it.

And now she was transforming right in front of him.

Panic gripped her. What was she going to do? What would happen if Cute Steve found out what she really was?

Her family had been very clear: do not let humans see your tail. Under any circumstances.

But then again, this might be the only time Cute Steve ever spoke to her. The only time! She couldn't let it go to waste, could she?

"So, are you doing anything fun this weekend?" she asked, right as her legs clamped together.

"Uh, I think we're going to Penalty's to watch a match."

Hopping frantically as though she were on a very wobbly pogo stick, Molly willed her skirt to stay in place. She fought the urge to cry out.

"Wonderful," she gasped. "Very nice. Sounds good!"

*Too many positive words, Molly! Talk like a normal human being, even if you can't walk like one!*

"What about you?" Cute Steve asked, kicking another stone and paying no attention to Molly's sudden breakdown. "Any fun parties?"

Astonished that Cute Steve thought she was the kind of person who had parties to go to, Molly tried to think of a funny response. Something punny?

Unfortunately, thinking was getting hard—she was starting to pant with the effort of remaining upright. She swung violently from side to side, like a jack-in-the-box. Even Cute Steve had started to look at her in bewilderment.

*Don't look down, don't look down, don't look down.*

"HeysorryIgottago," Molly garbled, now at a forty-five-degree angle to the ground.

Hopping like a lunatic, she burst through the fire exit to the swimming pool and ditched her backpack by the long tiled bench, where a bunch of puzzled sixth graders in rubber swimming caps sat watching her.

Still fully clothed, Molly leaped behind a wall of floatation devices. Although her shimmery white top and fully formed tail were shielded from view, she couldn't stay upright any longer, and she was about to topple to the ground. Just in time, she dived ungracefully into the deep end of the pool, plunging to the very bottom with a sigh of relief.

As soon as she was submerged, everything felt much

calmer, and she could breathe perfectly well—although the chlorine-infused water was much less pleasant to inhale than the tangy sea.

The temptation to stay at the bottom until the chaos subsided was strong, but she knew Ms. Phelps would dive in after her if she thought Molly was drowning. She had to resurface, but with a fresh wave of panic, Molly realized her tail was in full view.

*Quick! Think!*

What should she do?

Maybe if she thrashed her tail hard enough, the water would go foamy and opaque so that nobody would be able to make out the giant snowdrift she had instead of legs. It was worth a try.

Propelling herself to the surface, Molly shook the water from her eyes and, not making eye contact with the crowd of sixth graders, began swimming up and down the length of the swimming pool.

It was so *easy*. Molly had always been a good swimmer, but this was another level. Instead of half a minute, each length only took ten seconds, and with every stroke, she felt more and more powerful. After a few lengths of churning the water, she fell into an effortless rhythm, even doing those fancy underwater direction turns at each end. It felt as natural as breathing. It wasn't the crawl or breaststroke or butterfly or any of the other swimming techniques she'd been taught. This was something new entirely—something fluid and innate.

Even though she was filled with apprehension over what would happen when she stopped, Molly found she didn't ever *want* to stop. So she kept swimming, up and down like a shark, laser-focused and filled with powerful energy.

She was vaguely aware of the sixth graders dropping into the shallow end of the pool, vaguely aware of them plodding up and down doing a clumsy backstroke, vaguely aware of when they left again...and vaguely aware of Ms. Phelps crouching by the deep end, summoning Molly over.

Molly swished over to the edge of the pool and pressed her body flat against it so Ms. Phelps couldn't see her tail.

Ms. Phelps stared at her in astonishment. A plastic whistle hung loosely from her neck, and her straight blond hair was tied back in a neat bun. Her forearms were covered in colorful tattoos, including a pink dragon breathing blue fire. She was the youngest—and coolest—teacher in the school by far.

"Ms. Seabrook, that was...astounding. You're not even out of breath, are you?"

Molly shook her head. She wasn't breathless. Not in the slightest.

"Why have you been keeping this talent hidden?"

Molly shrugged. "Didn't want people to think I was weird." At least that part was true.

The teacher laughed. "Well, you've certainly made a splash today—in every sense! Maybe we could work on a smoother technique, although your unconventional style seems to be working for you. Would you be interested in joining the school swimming team?" Ms. Phelps smiled broadly, revealing a gap in her front teeth that somehow made her look even more friendly. "You're only in seventh grade, but you're absolutely strong enough to join the junior team at least. Would you like that?"

Molly's heart sank, because the second she realized she *would* like that was the same second she realized she could never do it. The possibility of hiding her tail from a whole bunch of teammates was zilch, no matter how badly she wanted to find a place she belonged.

Suddenly, the adrenaline from her epic swim session died. She felt deflated and sad all over again. "I'm sorry, Ms. Phelps. I don't think I can. But thank you."

After countless attempts at persuasion, Ms. Phelps eventually left Molly alone in the pool. Reluctantly, Molly climbed out—no mean feat when you have a giant tail that's useless on dry land—and dried herself off, then managed to wiggle back to the empty locker room, where she transformed back into a normal, boring, thirteen-year-old girl.

Frustration ebbed in Molly's chest as she trudged back up to the main school. She'd screwed up her one chance at ever holding a normal conversation with Cute Steve—the guy every girl in school would kill to be around. What if something romantic had started between them and she had ended up hanging out with the same people as Ada? They'd have to be friends again, then.

But no. What had *actually* happened was that she'd wobbled violently away from him as though she were on an exercise ball that was about to burst and dived into the swimming pool in front of a bunch of sixth graders. She'd have to come up with an excuse for missing her actual PE class too.

Fantastic. Being a freak had ruined everything, just like it always did.

# Carrot to Eagle

**M**ath class: also known as the place where dreams go to die.

Ms. Stavros, who had a well-known protractor obsession, explained acute angles for the ninetieth time. Molly had managed to nab a seat near Eddie of the Ears, but he was focusing all his energy on learning Pythagoras's theorem, which Molly found deeply offensive. How could triangles possibly be more interesting than her shark jokes?

A trapped fly buzzed inside the light fixture. Someone snored loudly from the back row, but Ms. Stavros was too busy fondling the swinging arms of a bevel protractor to notice. If news broke that Ms. Stavros had eloped with a pencil case and was expecting her first protractor child, Molly would have no difficulty believing it.

At one point, Ada half turned around and subtly looked

over her shoulder at Molly. Molly, who had already been staring at the back of her head, smiled weakly as they made eye contact. For a long second, Ada looked conflicted, unsure of whether to return the smile. She opted not to and turned back around. Molly's heart sank.

After the rest of math dragged by, it was time for biology, which was one of the few subjects Molly didn't actively hate. A lot of the other girls were squeamish during dissections, but Molly found them absolutely fascinating. Watching Mr. Moxton carve into a pig's heart to show them the different atria and ventricles gave her a strange kind of thrill, even though the smell was pretty gross.

Unfortunately, there was nothing to slice open today. Molly arrived in class to find they were being split into pairs to prepare presentations on food chains. This was the second most terrible news Molly had received all week, and it was about to get a whole lot worse, because they were split into pairs alphabetically. Which meant...

"Molly Seabrook and Ada Shen," Mr. Moxton called, sounding bored.

Ada groaned audibly. Molly wrapped her scarf tighter around the bottom half of her face in a bid to hide the frantic blushing. What had happened to the Ada who *almost* smiled at her earlier?

Then Molly realized Briony Tait, one of Felicity's friends, was in the class too. She'd been held back a year after a bad spell of mono wiped her out for most of the previous winter. So Ada was clearly trying to impress Briony, and it stung. Did she only want to be friends again when nobody popular was around?

Ada sidled over to Molly's bench space and dumped her new designer school bag on top of Molly's notes. She wrinkled her nose as though Molly were a bad smell.

"Right, let's get this over with." She flipped the laminated square of paper. "Our food chain is carrot to eagle."

Molly sighed. "Yeah. Any ideas?"

"Rabbits? Snakes? Rabbits definitely eat carrots, and snakes definitely eat rabbits, but what could come between snakes and eagles?"

"I have no idea," Molly admitted. She tried to make Ada laugh like she used to be able to do so easily. Maybe if she could break the ice that way, she'd be able to launch into an apology. "Buffalos? Aardvarks? Tasmanian devils?"

Ada sighed. "Could you actually try for once? Some of us actually *care* about our futures. We're not all planning to spend our lives in a chip shop."

Humiliation bubbled in Molly's veins. The desire to apologize evaporated.

To her surprise though, a clear voice piped up behind them: Eddie of the Ears. He was loosening his tie as though preparing for a fight. "I know I'd prefer working in a chip shop to being a boring accountant or whatever it is you plan on doing."

"Who even are you?" Ada snarked, even though she knew exactly who he was.

"I'm someone you can never be mean around," Eddie announced. "Because trust me, I will hear. My ears once landed me a job in a circus."

Ada folded her arms. "Circuses are inhumane."

"You're telling me!" Eddie agreed vigorously. "Once, my ears caused an accident and a bunch of other elephants got injured, so they made me dress up like a clown and perform dangerous stunts. Fortunately, my luck turned around when I discovered my ears gave me the power of flight, and I astounded everyone at the circus with my new talent."

There was a long pause. Then Ada said, "That's the plot of *Dumbo*."

"Which was loosely based on my life," Eddie said slowly, as though Ada were an idiot.

There was a tense silence, and Molly let out a peculiar little whimper, which she often did when she was trying desperately hard not to laugh.

To her enormous surprise, Ada let out a hearty bark of laughter, and before she knew it, the three of them were clutching their sides and cackling maniacally. Mr. Moxton helplessly tried to shush them, but it was no use. Tears streamed down Ada's face, and Molly's ribs ached. Eddie of the Ears had never looked more pleased with himself.

And it felt good. It felt really, really good to laugh with Ada again. But the moment didn't last, and when the laughter subsided, their fight had not been magically fixed.

From then on, Ada took charge of the presentation, kept Molly from contributing. When the bell finally rang, Ada started packing up her things in silence.

Molly didn't know whether it was the temporary bliss of laughing with her best friend again or the way Eddie of the Ears had the magical ability to make any situation feel less tense, but a sudden determination came over her.

She wanted Ada back in her life. She wanted it so badly. She wanted to tell her all about the insanity of the last few weeks, to gossip about Cute Steve and Penalty Pete, to discuss what subjects they'd drop the second they got the chance. To find out whether Ada still wanted to be a translator in the UN or whether she'd like to give accounting a shot after all.

And yet she'd screwed up. She'd screwed up badly. All right, so Ada had started the fight by gossiping about her to

Felicity, but Molly had made it go nuclear the second she'd brought up the divorce. It had been hugely unfair, and Molly hadn't meant a word of it, especially since Ada had been her rock during Mom's cancer diagnosis and treatment. Molly should be doing the same for Ada now while the breakup was still messy and the wounds were still raw.

The damage was done, but maybe it could be healed. Molly would never know unless she took the first step.

"Hey," she whispered to Ada, swallowing hard. "Can we talk?"

"I can't." Ada stuffed her leather pencil case into her backpack and hooked it over her dainty shoulder. "I'm meeting Pete at recess."

Molly noted the fact she no longer called him Penalty. Was this an attempt to make him seem cooler and more mature than he really was?

"Ada, please," Molly said, trying to keep the note of begging out of her voice. "I have something I want to say."

Ada started to walk away into the hallway.

"C'mon," Molly pleaded, jogging to keep up. Cute Steve looked over from the water fountain with interest, but Molly ignored the jittery feeling in her stomach. "We both said stuff we didn't mean. It wasn't just me, Ada, no matter how much you wish it was."

Ada sighed, strolling over to her locker and twiddling the padlock. She shoved her science textbooks on top of her gym clothes and slammed it shut again. "Whatever, Molly. I gotta go."

"Don't you miss having a best friend?" Molly asked, not even caring who heard now. "Because I know I do. Yeah, I have my sisters, and yeah, you have your new popular group. You have *Felicity*. But it's not the same. You know it's not. I bet none of them know about the time you baked your little brother's dirty diaper in the oven to punish your dad for grounding you."

Ada glared at Molly in horror, then shot Briony a don't-listen-to-this-weirdo look. "Molly, for God's sake. Don't—"

"Or the time you got taken to the emergency room because I poured sherbet in your ears on a dare."

"Molly, stop..." Ada said, but her lips twitched at the memory. Something in her hard stare softened.

Molly barreled onward. "Or the time you laughed so hard at my fake Russian accent you did farts that sounded like a machine gun."

Ada giggled now, covering her face with her hands. "OK, OK, I give up—"

"In fact, I'm not convinced you didn't follow through," Molly added. "You disappeared to the bathroom *very* quickly."

Ada snorted. "Do you really wanna play this game, Little

Miss Dialed 911 About a Pigeon You Were Convinced Was Stalking You?"

"In my defense," Molly replied in a faux haughty tone, "my grandpa always said he would be reincarnated as a pigeon. I genuinely thought I was being haunted."

"So you called the police."

"I tried the Ghostbusters first, but they were swamped."

Ada was truly belly laughing now, and it felt even better than before, because this time, Molly had made it happen.

When they finally calmed down, Ada threw her arms around Molly, her citrusy perfume smell familiar and comforting. "I'm sorry, Molls. You know I love the chip shop. We've had to go to Finnegan's Fish for weeks. Their curry sauce is awful."

"Traitor!" Molly said. "I take back my apology."

Ada frowned. "You didn't apologize."

"Oh yeah." Molly suddenly felt awkward again, but this time, it'd be easier to say it and mean it, because it wasn't falling on deaf ears. "I'm sorry, Ada. Really. And I'm also sorry your parents are such giant buttholes."

Ada rolled her eyes. "Me too. So what's been going on with you?"

Molly opened her mouth to answer but quickly clamped it shut again. Even though she really wasn't supposed to, she desperately wanted to tell Ada about the tail, about mermaids, about this whole other life she never knew she had. About transforming in front of Cute Steve and wobbling around like she was on a pogo stick.

But how would Ada react? She'd probably think Molly was teasing her or trying to make her look like an idiot. Or just outright lying for attention. After all, who in their right mind genuinely believed mermaids were real? And if Ada *did* believe her, she'd just be reminded of how much of a freak Molly was. How inescapably weird her family was. If she couldn't handle the grease smell, how on earth could she accept this?

Muttering half-heartedly, Molly said, "Didn't you say you had to go and meet Penalty Pete?"

"Nah." Ada scrunched up her petite nose. "He talks about nothing but soccer. Just, like, constantly. Pete, what would you like for lunch? The World Cup. Great. With fries?"

Molly cackled, her best friend's sarcasm music to her ears after so long without it. They walked side by side to their favorite bench by the soccer field and spent the rest of morning recess catching up as though nothing had ever happened between them.

But something *had* happened. To Molly, anyway. And as she looked at the rain clouds gathering ominously overhead, she couldn't help but wonder how long she could possibly keep it a secret.

# Purple Tail

*A*nother night, another boardwalk shift. Since it was drizzling lightly and the haddock suit was not waterproof, it really should've been a miserable evening. But somehow, it wasn't, because Ada was back in Molly's life, and everything felt lighter and brighter because of it.

Molly made a solemn promise to herself never to let her hot temper get the better of her again. She would never let her quick mouth ruin any of the other relationships in her life. Of course, this was a promise she had made to herself many times before, but she was sure that this time, it would stick. She just had to think before she spoke and not make rash decisions in the heat of the moment.

Except when it came to the snotty old lady who'd called the police on her mom. When Molly saw the ancient biddy strolling toward her haddocky spot on the boardwalk, the sinister little gremlin in Molly's heart reared its ugly head. *Trip her up*, it whispered, cackling evilly. *Whip her with your tail. Push her out to sea like a Viking burial.*

Somehow, Molly managed to refrain from all of the above and felt a swell of pride as she smiled politely at the woman. She was practically a saint.

When the time came to close up the shop, Mom entrusted Margot and Melissa with the task. Molly wiped down all the counters and mopped the floors, suspecting that she had gotten the raw end of the deal.

"Sooo," Margot said, tapping her foot in time with the radio as she jotted some numbers into columns. "How do you feel about sneaking down to Coley Cavern tonight?"

Molly swallowed. Although she found herself craving the peace of mind she got from spending time as a mermaid, she just wanted to focus on the real world. Now that she had Ada back as a friend and Cute Steve had willingly exchanged non-onion-ring words with her, she felt like those were the things she should be paying most attention to. "Nah, not tonight. I'm sorry."

Margot's eyes twinkled. "Myla's meeting someone. I want to know who."

"Margot!" Melissa snapped, dumping the bank bag of

change onto the table with a clatter. "Don't gossip like that!" She turned to where Molly was mopping and put on her best prim-teacher frown. "Molly, it's *really* none of our business who Myla spends her time with. Don't let Margot—"

"How do you know she's meeting someone?" Molly asked Margot, ignoring Melissa's rant.

Margot's lip twitched. "Melissa was taking a big bath and overheard Myla on the phone, planning a meet-up."

"Like...a *romantic* thing?" Molly had never considered Myla to be a person with a love life before. The thought was very strange, like imagining a moth having a crush on someone.

Margot shrugged, then snapped an elastic band around a stack of bills. "Well, Myla insisted to Melissa that it wasn't, but you know what Melissa's merpower is..."

"Myla was lying?"

"Bingo!"

Melissa abandoned the pile of twenties she was counting and yelled, "*Margot!* I knew I should never have told you."

"But you did," Margot pointed out. "So this is really on you. Whaddaya say, Molly?"

Melissa grabbed her head in her hands and screamed at the top of her lungs. "Arrrghhh!"

"Dude, what's your trout?" Molly asked innocently.

Melissa whipped around to face her. "My trout, Molly, is

that you and Margot *never* listen to what I have to say. Ever. You're both *horrible*. You just barge into everything without thinking it through and then come crying to me when you mess it up. I'm sick of it. I'm sick of *you*."

Molly wiped her brow on her sleeve. "You just spat on me. Why does your spit smell like cheeseburgers? You're supposed to be vegetarian."

"Stop it! Just stop it! Stop trying to be like Margot with the endless jokes and just be a decent human being for once!" With that, Melissa leaped to her feet and stormed from the shop, the door banging shut behind her. The bell whimpered pathetically.

Molly winced. "I kind of feel like we shouldn't go."

"Coward," Margot snorted. "Pleeease. Why don't we try to find out what your merpower is at the same time? Aren't you curious?"

"Not really," Molly lied.

"What if it's something amazing? Like time travel? Or mind control? Or... Oh my God, what if it's *flying*?"

Molly's mental image of a teenage mermaid hurtling through the sky alongside two jumbo jets and a goose formation was really something.

Slapping the wet mop against the tiles, Molly sighed. "Fine. If only to get you to shut up."

But the truth was, she *was* curious about her merpower. It could be any of those epic things Margot just mentioned, or it could be something even better. Like fireballs, for instance. Although that might not be the most useful ability to have while underwater.

Myla had arranged to meet her mystery date at midnight, so at eleven thirty, Molly and Margot slipped down into the kitchen, shifted the broken dishwasher, and climbed down into the cellar. Since Myla had no idea about the secret trapdoor, there was no chance of running into her at the wrong moment.

The smell of dusty books hit Molly as they descended the wooden ladder, and again there was a longing tug in her chest. Maybe one day she would sneak down here alone and flip through some of the antique tomes.

In particular, she had her sights set on one called *Ancient Mermaid Rituals for Manifesting Love and Desire*. If she could find some weird old spell to magic Cute Steve into liking her, her life would become a lot easier. And if she got caught breaking into his house to smear a love heart of squid ink on his bare chest, she could just say she'd had too much sea air; she wasn't sure "I'm a mermaid and this is what we do" would be a valid legal defense.

The two sisters transformed in silence as Margot wound

open the giant hole in the floor, and this time, Molly relished the jump into the sea. For those few split seconds before she hit the water, she felt weightless and free, like the moment a roller coaster just begins to drop.

The sea itself was even better. Crisp and fresh, the saltwater was delicious in her gills. As she swam down to the cavern, her muscles felt like they were finally being used in the right way—giving her a sensation of deep satisfaction, like a really good stretch first thing in the morning.

Coley Cavern was much quieter than the last time they were there, mainly because it was nearly midnight and there had been no clamdunk game that evening. The ancient merman clutching a giant spear—Old Alan—was still napping on the sand. Although briefly tempted to prod him with a stick to make sure he was still breathing, Molly was relieved when he let out an almighty snore, even if it was rather like a small earthquake as it echoed around the cavern.

There was also a group of mermen in their early twenties practicing clamdunk trick shots—was one of them Myla's date?—and a slightly younger mermaid with pale skin, long ginger hair, and a beautiful purple tail. She was perched on a rock and reading a book. Molly wondered how on earth she'd gotten it here without the pages getting wet.

"Right, so what do we do now?" Molly asked. "Wait

behind a rock until Myla shows up?" She tried to tread water, then realized she was kind of floating without having to do much. Tails were weird.

Margot thought about this. "Now would be a really good time to see if your merpower is invisibility. Quick, just concentrate on it really hard."

"What do you mean?"

Her sister shrugged, squeezing the excess water from her curly hair. "Think about how it feels to be invisible and see if anything happens."

"I've never been invisible before," Molly muttered. "How would I know what it feels like?"

"Er... Use your imagination?"

So Molly focused very hard on the feeling she had whenever Cute Steve was in the room. Like she wasn't even there and was just watching him from the other side of a TV screen. Like she didn't really exist. That was as close to invisibility as she ever got.

However, she didn't feel any tingling of power beneath her skin, and when she looked down, her arms were in full view. "Nope. It's not invisibility."

Margot tutted. "Right. Hiding behind a rock it is. How unoriginal."

It didn't take long for Myla to arrive. She burst through

the surface in the middle of the cavern, shook her sleek black hair, and swam across to the shore.

Margot nudged Molly excitedly. Myla was swimming in the direction of where the group of guys were playing clamdunk, but at the last second, she stopped at the rock where the purple-tailed mermaid was reading her book. Purple Tail looked up and smiled as Myla approached, then laid down her book on the slippery rock. She offered Myla a hand out of the water, and Myla accepted.

"Now that's a plot twist," Margot whispered.

Molly watched as her older sister nestled next to Purple Tail and started chatting contentedly. They looked comfortable and familiar with each other—this was no first date. Molly's suspicions were confirmed when Myla pecked Purple Tail sweetly on the lips, and Purple Tail giggled happily.

"*Wait*," Margot murmured. "That's... Oh my God, that's Amy Fairbairn!"

"The girl from senior year?"

Margot nodded triumphantly. "The one and only. Myla must've lied when she said she had no idea Amy was a mermaid."

The two younger sisters watched as Myla started to read Amy's book over her shoulder, one arm wrapped around Amy's curvy waist.

"I'm kind of mad she didn't tell us," Margot muttered.

"Well, we do sort of make fun of everything," Molly pointed out.

"But we'd never make fun of this!"

Molly folded her arms. "And yet it's fine for you to make fun of me for being interested in Cute Steve."

Margot looked at her, aghast. "You did not, in all seriousness, just call him Cute Steve."

Blushing furiously, Molly forgot that she only ever called him that to Ada. She changed the subject somewhat. "I mean, you never talk about your love life either, Margs. None of us do. Except maybe Minnie, but hers is largely unicorn-based."

Margot shrugged but didn't meet Molly's eye. "I'm just not that interested in boys. Or girls. Or anyone. Not like that, anyway. I just like pranking people. I don't want to have to kiss them or anything." She shuddered as though she couldn't think of anything worse. "Do you?"

"Yes," Molly replied. "Definitely. Just nobody with lip fillers."

"Maybe there's something wrong with me." Margot sounded unsure of herself for probably the first time in her life, and it caught Molly off guard. Margot was the most confident person Molly knew. It was weird to hear her doubt herself.

"There are many things wrong with you," Molly agreed, "but your lack of interest in kissing is not one of them."

Margot smiled at that. "I think we should go."

"Me too." Molly watched Myla tuck a wet lock of hair behind Amy's ear and grinned. She was seeing a different side to all her sisters tonight. Maybe they'd go home and find Melissa breaking the law or clog dancing.

"Wait!" Margot said suddenly. "We should test to see if your merpower is teleportation."

"Good point," Molly said. She closed her eyes and focused very hard on Kittiwake Keep.

Maybe too hard.

Margot pointed at the stream of bubbles that popped to the surface behind Molly. "Did you just concentrate so hard you farted?"

"Shut up," said Molly.

## CHAPTER

# 16

......................

# *Mashed Peas*

The next morning, waking up was a heroic effort. Only Molly's rumbling stomach roused her from her warm bed. As she buttered and jammed a doorstop wedge of toast, Melissa appeared at the kitchen door in her fluffy bathrobe and boiled the kettle.

"Cup of tea?" Melissa asked. Molly was surprised to be offered one after the storming fight they'd had the day before.

"Please," she replied cautiously, as though her sister was a wildebeest she didn't want to startle into a stampede.

Slowly, though, the two started talking again. This was what always seemed to happen when Molly had a falling-out with any of her siblings. There was rarely an official apology. Things just automatically went back to normal without anyone making the conscious effort to kiss and make up.

Molly was fairly sure she could murder their aunt Maureen over breakfast and her sisters would all be talking to her again over lunch.

Early that morning, Myla and their mom had left for Prescott University, where they were spending the weekend exploring before Myla's college interview the following Monday. Molly was secretly glad—there was no way she'd have been able to resist asking Myla about Purple Tail, aka Amy Fairbairn.

Aunt Maureen volunteered to run the chip shop in Mom's absence, which was terrible news for the remaining Seabrook sisters. Their aunt was famous for making them keep the shop open as late as possible so they'd capture the crowds leaving the bar around the corner. Molly was a little put off by bar patrons after the time an extremely drunk old lady had tried to eat the fins on her haddock suit, but there was simply no telling Aunt Maureen.

While Mom was warm and kind, Maureen was the polar opposite—stern, austere, and hard around the edges. Margot explained to Molly that this was because Aunt Maureen was also a mermaid but never spent *any* time in the water, so she was taut with tension and bitterness.

Plus, she'd always resented the fact that Molly's grand-father had left the chip shop to Mom when he'd passed away ten years ago. Molly strongly suspected Aunt Maureen would truly like Mom and all the Seabrook sisters to drown in a flash flood so she could finally run the place her way.

Once, Molly had a bronchial infection and tried to get off work under Aunt Maureen's watch. "Nothing I hate more than people who are lazy and no-shows," Aunt Maureen had barked down the phone. "Work-shy, the whole group of you. When I was your age, I was down working in the mines every weekend, influenza or not."

Molly highly doubted this was true, but she knew how much adults loved to talk about how much worse they'd had it back in their day, so she'd stayed silent.

Today, despite her tiredness, Molly reluctantly agreed to a shift working behind the counter. Even though *technically* she wasn't supposed to serve people until she was fourteen, Aunt Maureen was not overly concerned with petty things like law and order. Molly was grateful for the break from the Good Ship Haddock, so she didn't like to argue. In any case, Molly thought it highly unlikely that police would storm the place looking for underage fish fryers. Not when they were such loyal customers themselves.

The chip shop was always jammed on a Saturday, and the shift was passing by pretty quickly. Working alongside Margot was always fun, thanks to her silly dances, goofy jokes, and elaborate pranks. For example, today she had stuffed mini marshmallows into all the jumbo straws on the counter and was hooting with laughter as a petulant child kept declaring them all broken.

Scoffing, Aunt Maureen began changing the oil in the fryer. "For goodness' sake, girls, you're teenagers now. Really, you must start behaving like ladies. It's not attractive to carry on like this."

Margot looked like she might be on the brink of pointing out that Aunt Maureen had never attracted anyone in her life, but Molly shot her a warning glance. It was always worth keeping their aunt from losing it completely.

Molly was in the middle of replenishing the sausages in the counter display when she saw something that made her heart sink through the floor.

Ada and Cute Steve were walking past the window, side by side, arms brushing together, and Ada giggling up at his handsome face.

The intense wave of jealousy caught Molly off guard. She couldn't help but feel hurt by the sight of her best friend and the guy she liked walking together.

The sensible side of her brain told her it was probably innocent—Ada quizzing Cute Steve about what to get Pete for his birthday or something. And it wasn't like anything was ever going to happen between Molly and Cute Steve. Especially now that he was dating Felicity.

Maybe what got to Molly was the feeling of missing out. She often felt a little jealous of her friends who didn't have jobs. They could spend their evenings and weekends doing whatever they liked. Their parents would give them an allowance for important things like ice cream and skateboards or whatever cool people spent their money on. Molly found herself wishing she could spend her Saturday strolling around on the boardwalk, playing games in the amusement arcade, and wandering around the shops looking for a new outfit to wear.

Molly shook away the jolt of self-pity as best she could. The most important thing right now was that Ada was back in her life. She desperately wanted to keep it that way.

The main highlight of the day was Eddie of the Ears, who came in for his chips and fried pieces around lunchtime. His maroon beanie was pulled down so low that only his generous lobes could be seen poking out of the bottom.

What hilarious thing was he going to say today? She could really use a good laugh.

However, Eddie of the Ears looked deeply worried as he asked, voice low, "Is everything OK?"

Was her sadness over Cute Steve and Ada and endless

chip-shop shifts that obvious? Swallowing hard and faking a bright smile, Molly said, "Why wouldn't it be?"

Eddie lowered his voice even further. "I heard there was a fight down here last night."

Molly frowned in confusion. "A...fight?" Had he heard Melissa's screeching?

"Yeah." Eddie's lobes twitched, which is apparently a thing among the generously eared of this world. "Two fish got battered and the chips were a-salted."

Molly groaned, but she instantly relaxed. "Eddie, this is not the time or plaice to be joking."

Now he looked genuinely worried. "Oh. Sorry."

"No...*plaice*." She tried to explain her dreadful pun. "As in...the fish. Maybe that's more of a written joke."

"Hey," he snickered. "I guess your sense of humor is just too advanced for lowly nerds like me."

"What can I get for you?"

"Three sausages and mashed peas."

"Seriously?"

"No. Chips and fried pieces. Peas and thank you."

Putting on her most serious expression, Molly sighed and said, "Look, by law, I must ask you whether you would really like mashed peas."

Eddie of the Ears blinked. "By law?"

"We take misuse of side dishes very seriously, Edward."

Faux horrified, Eddie clutched his hand to his chest. "Oh, you did *not* just Edward me."

Unfortunately, preparing Eddie's chips and fried pieces only took a few seconds, and before Molly knew it, he was waving goodbye again. She found herself wishing he could've stayed longer and then wondering why she wished that when Cute Steve was *clearly* her soul mate.

Boys were confusing. So were feelings. Molly thought life would be a lot easier if neither existed at all.

# Baboon Buttholes

On Sunday morning, Molly was awakened by a thump on the bedroom door. Aunt Maureen shoved it open, tossed the house phone at her, and said, "Ada somebody."

After spending so long worrying she'd ruined their friendship forever, the moment sent a burst of warmth through Molly's chest. She vowed never to take her friendship with Ada for granted again and almost considered pitching some kind of blood-brother pact to Ada in order to make it permanent.

"Hi!" Molly said, fighting the urge to yawn. She was still catching up on sleep from Friday night's Coley Cavern antics.

"Hey! You weren't answering your phone, so I rang the landline. It felt very retro. Maybe tomorrow, I'll send a telegram." Ada's voice was chirpy and fast. "Anyway, I have my cousins visiting from Chenzhou, and we're road-tripping to the zoo. There's a sunset penguin parade. Do you wanna tag along with Minnie? She's always pestering you to take her to see the gorillas, right?"

"Baboons," Molly corrected her. "She likes buttholes. Especially red ones."

Ada snorted. "I think that's a Seabrook thing. So what do you think? Are you in?"

"I think Minnie has a birthday party to go to, but I'm definitely in!"

"Sweet. I'll pick you up at one. Bring snacks."

It was Margot and Melissa's turn to work in the chip shop with Aunt Maureen that day, so the two went off for their shift, and Molly set up at the kitchen table with the stacks of homework she'd let pile up over the last week.

Molly hated homework. She would rather dance around in the haddock suit for ten straight hours than do one sheet of math equations. Her attention span was roughly that of a teaspoon, and trying to focus on one thing for hours at a time was almost impossible.

There was a boy in her year at school who had ADHD, and Molly was pretty sure they shared the exact same symptoms. But she didn't want to make a fuss by forcing her mom to book a doctor's appointment, and she certainly didn't want to risk anyone mocking her for it. So she powered through with algebra despite the entertaining diversions her brain was performing for her right at that very moment.

As she worked, her mind drifted over and over to Cute Steve. Maybe now that Ada and Molly were friends again and Ada was going out with Penalty Pete, Molly would have the chance to roll in the popular circle and woo Cute Steve with her unbelievable charm and wit. All she had to do was practice making actual words with her mouth—she wasn't keen to relive the "glumph" fiasco, since the odds of Cute Steve being romantically attracted to bullfrogs was very slim.

Of course, Molly wasn't the only person at school to have a crush on Cute Steve. In fact, it would be easier to count the people who *didn't*. And there was the problem that Cute Steve was already dating a kitchen table, i.e. Felicity of the Fillers. But in Molly's elaborate wooing fantasies, this didn't matter. After all, none of those other kids—not even Felicity—knew Cute Steve's onion ring preferences, so Molly was at a clear advantage.

It was just before midday when old Aunt Reeny barged back into the Keep, waking up a snoozing Molly, who was drooling over a diagram of a volcano.

"What is it, Dory?" Molly moaned, still half asleep, words slurpy and sticky from the saliva pooling in the corner of her mouth.

"Up!" barked Aunt Maureen, arms folded crossly. "You're needed."

"I... What?" Molly mumbled, rubbing her eyes and dabbing her slobber on the tablecloth.

"I have to run an errand. I need you to go to work for a few hours."

Molly fought the urge to pout. "But I have plans with Ada. We're going to the zoo."

Aunt Maureen zipped up her raincoat. It smelled like a stable, even though she'd never been near a horse in her life. "That will have to wait."

"That's not fair," Molly complained. "You can't expect me to drop everything just because you have to go to the post office or whatever." Or the coven of evil witches and warlocks, she wanted to say, which seemed more likely.

"I can, and I do. I am the adult and you are the child, and you will do as I say while I am living in this house."

"Seriously, I can't," Molly tried feebly. "I haven't finished my homework."

A disdainful head shake. "You shouldn't have left it to the last minute."

"Maybe I wouldn't have needed to if I didn't have to work all the time," Molly pointed out, and then Aunt Maureen was off again, going on about how much better behaved schoolchildren were when there was a spanking involved. Molly couldn't help but fantasize about spanking Aunt Maureen's—

"Fine," Molly said, slamming her textbook shut with resignation. "I'll go to work."

"Good. And don't even think about closing early. Susan and Keith from across the street will be watching. They have me on speed dial in case you try anything...funny."

Heart sinking with disappointment, Molly called Ada back.

She picked up on the second ring. "Hey! So I know I said bring snacks, but I already got potato chips, gummy bears, and white chocolate popcorn. *White chocolate popcorn*, Molly! Can you believe this is a thing? Have I just changed your life? I feel like I might've just changed your life."

If Molly wasn't feeling disappointed before, she certainly was now. She felt like a toddler, but tears pricked at her eyes. She wanted to go so badly. Penguins, popcorn, and Ada were three of her very favorite things, and work was making her miss out *again*.

"I'm so sorry, Ads. My aunt is making me work. I can't come anymore."

Ada's upbeat tone vanished. "Oh. OK."

"I'm sorry." Molly's gut squirmed uncomfortably, praying

her best friend wouldn't hate her all over again. "I really do want to come."

"Yeah, I know." Ada's voice was as flat as a pancake that had been run over by a steamroller. "Don't worry. I'll invite Pete."

ℓ·ℓ·ℓ

At work, Molly slammed around the shop so angrily that the cash register drawer snapped off its hinges. Margot hastily removed her from the front counter and told her to take over kebab duty. Molly hated slicing kebabs, because when the meat cylinder got really small and skinny, you ended up cooking your knuckles against the grill. But still, it was much easier to vent your world-ending rage when you had a stinking hunk of factory-floor meat to take it out on.

At quarter to one, a familiar voice appeared in front of the counter. Molly turned from the kebab to see Eddie of the Ears standing there, grinning sheepishly. Margot had conveniently gone to the bathroom the moment he stepped through the door, leaving Molly to serve him alone.

"I came by earlier for chips and fried pieces," Eddie of the Ears said, rubbing the back of his neck. "But, uh, you weren't here. So I decided to have a later lunch instead."

Molly grinned. "My sisters could've served you."

Eddie of the Ears shook his head in dismissal. "They don't do it right. The fried pieces aren't fried enough."

"I'll let them know." Molly snorted and started preparing his lunch.

"Everything OK?" he asked, watching her scoop the crispy slivers of salty batter onto a huge box of fresh chips. "You seem a little downbeat. Or worried. Or maybe ecstatic. I'm not good with reading body language. You might've just won the lottery and I'd say sorry for your loss."

Molly laughed, but even she could tell the sound was half-hearted. "Yeah, I'm fine. Annoyed I have to work. There was something I was supposed to do. And now I can't."

Cautiously, Eddie of the Ears asked, "A date?"

"Pffft. No. Going to examine baboon bottoms at the zoo."

"The finest of Sunday-afternoon activities." Eddie chuckled. "Anything I can do?"

Molly finished wrapping the chips and fried pieces in newspaper, then rang them through the register. It sputtered angrily when it tried to open the broken change drawer. "Not unless you'd be interested in covering my shift."

Eddie shrugged. "Sure."

"Good one."

"No, really. I can do it."

"No, you can't."

"Why not?" he asked, shrugging again. "I come in here often enough to know the menu top to bottom. How much skill does it take to batter a cod?"

Molly rolled her eyes. "You'd be surprised."

"Good thing I'm a fast learner."

"See, now I'm starting to think you're not joking."

Eddie laughed. "I'm not. For once."

Molly stared at him, stunned by his insane levels of kindness. "You'd actually do that?"

"What was it you said back on your birthday? 'You can have my job if you want. All the free chips and fried pieces you can eat.' This is just me making good on your offer. Nothing to do with helping you out. I'm just in it for the free food. I spend so much on chips and fried pieces that I'm considering renting out my bedroom to help with the cost."

Molly couldn't believe it. She genuinely couldn't believe it. How was anyone so ridiculously nice?

"Thanks, Eddie of the Ears," she choked out, a lump forming in her throat.

"I think you mean Eddie of the Eddie."

"Yeah, that one. Give me a sec to run this by my sisters?"

"No problem. Mom's parked outside. I'll go and tell her I'll be a while."

Before the deluge of tears got the better of her, she pushed into the kitchen and hastily filled in Margot and Melissa on this remarkable update. They stared at her in astonishment, waiting for the punchline, then when they realized none was coming, they seemed genuinely happy for her. They promised to help Eddie as best they could, and if Aunt Maureen came back in a hissy fit of rage, they'd tie her to the deep-fat fryer and roast her until she shut up.

By the time Molly reappeared out front, she had the crying under control and was all business. Dragging Eddie back into the kitchen so they were out of sight, she grabbed the cap off her head and handed it to him. "Here, switch hats with me."

Eddie, to his credit, did not question this, just handed over his beloved beanie and yanked the cap over his ears as best he could. "You have a really big head," he said as his eyes disappeared underneath the hat.

Molly pulled the warm beanie, which smelled of green apple shampoo, over her head. It was indeed very tight. "Maybe you just have a really *small* head."

Eddie of the Ears nodded. "Or we're both freaks."

"Probably that one. Listen, you're going to need to act as me-like as possible."

Eddie peered up at her from underneath the overwhelmingly large cap. "What? Why?"

159

"Susan and Keith across the street. They have binoculars pointed at the shop front right now."

"That's not creepy at all."

"My aunt's way of checking up on us. You're wearing black, and you're the same height as me, so they *might* not notice. But just in case, do your best me impression."

Eddie tilted his chin up defiantly, squared his shoulders, and fixed a look of vague anger on his face. "Hello, I'm Molly. Buy my chips or I'll murder your family."

Molly burst out laughing, forgetting to even be offended. "Perfect. Thanks, Eddie of the Eddie."

"No problem, Molly of the Neptune Head."

CHAPTER

## 18

# The Biggest Spectacle at the Zoo

The zoo was cast in a warm glow from the late autumn sun, but the air had a chilly tinge. Molly and Ada's family were all wrapped up in boots and overcoats, as were most visitors, but there were still the occasional weirdos wearing shorts and flip-flops as they ogled the lions in their enclosures. *Ah, by the sea*, thought Molly. *Where people wear cargo shorts during a blizzard, just because they like the pockets.*

They'd driven half an hour to get there, and Molly was dying to tell Ada about what Eddie of the Ears had done for her. Instead, she made polite conversation with Ada's dad and uncle and tried not to be sick when Ada's five-year-old cousin blew a snot bubble in her face. It was just about endurable when Minnie did gross things, because she was Molly's flesh and blood, but there was something so unbelievably disgusting about other kids.

Eventually, they made it to the zoo, bought their tickets, then strolled around the monkey house as they waited for the sun to set and the penguins to parade. As they walked, Molly and Ada dropped back to gossip about Eddie of the Ears' remarkable goodwill.

Ada was still bouncing and fizzing, as she had been since Molly phoned to tell her she was coming after all, but smiled warmly as Molly recounted the story. "I can't believe he did that for you."

"I know," Molly agreed. "It's wild." And yet, she *could* believe that he'd done it, because he was just that kind of person. Sweet and caring without expecting anything in return.

Molly *would* return it, though. Somehow, she'd find a favor of equal value. Not just because she hated feeling like she owed people something but also because she found herself genuinely wanting to do something good for the boy with the overwhelming lobes.

She wanted to discuss Eddie of the Ears with Ada some more, but the youngest cousin—five-year-old Li Jun, of snot-bubble fame—came dancing over to them. His older brother Zhang Yong came close behind. He seemed to consider himself his little brother's babysitter, and it was sweet for Molly to see. It reminded her of how Margot used to be with her when they were little.

"Hey, kiddo," Ada said, ruffling Li Jun's thick black hair. "If you could be any animal in the world, what would you be?"

Li Jun hopped excitedly from foot to foot. "A chimp."

"Are you just saying that because you're looking at chimps right now?"

A somber gorilla made eye contact with Molly. Its eyes were deep and sad. Molly suddenly realized how much she hated zoos. What if the human world found out about mermaids? Would *she* be kept in a cage for people to ogle while they ate cotton candy and took pictures?

Li Jun shrugged. "Maybe."

Molly folded her arms. "If you were looking at an earthworm, would you want to be an earthworm?"

"*No*," Li Jun said emphatically. "Because earthworms aren't real. I'm not *stupid*."

Zhang Yong gave Molly and Ada a knowing look, as if to say they just let him have this moment. Zhang Yong was only eight but wise beyond his years. So...maybe not that much like Margot.

"Right, of course." Ada nodded. "Mol, what about you?"

Molly shrugged. "Probably a leopard. They're awesome."

"I thought you'd want to be something oceany. Like a dolphin or a whale."

"That's very narrow-minded of you."

Ada laughed and linked her arm through Molly's. She hadn't done that in forever, and it made Molly grin. "I'm so happy you're here, not Penalty Pete." Ada sighed. "If I asked him what kind of animal he'd want to be, he'd probably say Gareth Southgate."

Molly frowned. "Who's that?"

"I really have no idea. Something to do with the World Cup. I try not to listen when Pete talks."

They watched as one chimp smacked another one around the head with a banana skin. It was like a live-action cartoon. "So do you think you'll break up with him?"

Ada chewed her lip. "I don't know. What are you supposed to do when the things you thought you wanted turn out to be kind of a mistake?"

"Admit you were wrong and move on?"

A meaningful pause. "But he's such a good kisser."

"Oh my God," Molly squealed. "You've *kissed*? I need to know *everything*! First—"

"Keep it down," Ada muttered, smiling genially at her dad, who had turned around at the sound of Molly's banshee wailing.

"Right, sorry," Molly mumbled hastily. "But what kind of texture do boys' tongues have? Is it the same as ours? Or more...sandpapery? I imagine it to be like putting a starfish in your mouth."

"Eurgh," Li Jun said, wrinkling his nose. "That's *gross*. Why would you put a starfish in your mouth?"

Ada laughed, then whispered to Molly, "I'll tell you every tiny detail the second my little cousins aren't hanging on my every word."

"OK," announced Ada's dad. "We need to find a spot for the sunset penguin parade."

Zhang Yong frowned as they exited the monkey house. "It looks pretty busy."

"Why don't you kids go on ahead?" said Ada's uncle. "We'll wait for you in the café." He winked at Ada's dad. Molly suspected they might sell beer in the café.

"Good idea," Ada said, turning to Molly. "Tell you what, Mol. I'll go this way with Zhang Yong and Li Jun. You go that way and see if there's more space toward the finish line. Text me if you find a spot, OK?"

Molly wandered away from the monkey house and toward the finish line for the penguin parade. The sugary scent of cotton candy was in the air, and the chirping of parrots could be heard over the chattering excitement of the crowd preparing for the parade. Molly felt happier than she had in a long time and couldn't help smiling as she walked around the perimeter of the penguin trail.

Zhang Yong was right, though. It was very busy. There were no spare benches anywhere, nor were there any standing spaces on the route the penguins would take. The grassy banks were covered in people.

She walked farther and farther toward the finish line, but it was no use. Unless she found some form of stepladder or stilts, there was no way they'd be able to see the emperor penguin leading his pals around the park.

Unfortunately, the crowd was so packed that Molly didn't quite realize how close she was getting to the penguin enclosure.

The whiff of kippers on the breeze was the first clue, and the excited squeals from toddlers was the second.

And then she turned into a mermaid.

CHAPTER

## 19

# Do Penguins Bark?

**M**olly's eyes blurred with panic as she felt the unmistakable tingle of a mermaid tail materializing.

*Oh God. Oh God, oh God, oh GOD!*

The sidewalk around her was mobbed with people setting up tripods and checking maps. On one side was a grassy bank covered in picnickers, and on the other was the outer fence of the penguin enclosure. Inside, the penguins were barking.

Do penguins bark? Molly did not know and could not think, because she was too busy *transforming into a mermaid in front of hundreds of people.*

She had to think fast—and find some cover. There was a short line of refreshment and gift kiosks in front of the enclosure fence with a tight gap behind them. Maybe if she could hurl herself behind there...

But then she'd be even closer to the lake in the penguin enclosure, and transforming back into a human being would be impossible.

Her jeans began to disappear. Her legs cemented together.

The kiosk solution wasn't perfect, but it was her only option. Mere seconds before the scales appeared and her tail materialized, Molly dove behind the T-shirt stall with an *oooft*.

Panting hard, she struggled to turn herself over so she was facing the sky, not the ground. She was wedged in there pretty snugly. The penguins barked mockingly. She found herself getting irrationally annoyed with them.

At least she was shielded from view, and she didn't think anyone had seen her clumsy leap.

*Why me?* Molly thought miserably. Just when she was starting to come to terms with being an unbelievable freak, something like this happened and made her furious all over again.

It wasn't fair. Why couldn't she just enjoy a trip to the zoo like a normal thirteen-year-old—without having to sneak out of a stupid chip shop and worry about turning into a *mermaid* along the way?

Staring at the sky in resignation, she fought the urge to cry. Frustration always made her feel like this. She could handle sadness or anger without bursting into tears, but the second something frustrated her, her tear ducts became Niagara Falls.

The penguin parade was about to start. The trainers herded the peculiar little birds into a neat row at the entrance, like when teachers make elementary school kids pair up and hold hands to walk anywhere.

What was she going to do? She'd have to wait here until the zoo had emptied. Ada and her family would either be worried sick or incredibly irritated.

Fishing her phone out of her backpack, she fired off a text to Ada.

Stuck in the bathroom. Must've eaten some bad chips.
Will be back once the stomach settles.

Hopefully, Ada would be so uncomfortable over the phrase "stomach settles" that she wouldn't come looking for her.

A ripple of cheers erupted as the penguins began their parade around the zoo circuit. Elated laughter from toddlers mingled with delighted squeals from teenagers and rowdy clapping from parents. Molly no longer had a view of the parade, so she decided to focus all her attention on thinking her way out of this current bind.

She seemed to be stuck behind a T-shirt kiosk that sold kitschy animal-themed apparel and umbrellas. The back of it had a door for the staff to get in and out of, and it was currently slightly ajar.

Molly could hear the unmistakable iPhone keyboard taps coming from inside the kiosk, so clearly the zoo employee was using the penguin parade as an opportunity to catch up on their correspondence.

Maybe if she could open the door wide enough to grab some T-shirts, she could fashion some kind of sarong to cover her tail? All right, so it was *technically* theft, but she would return the T-shirts once she was back in the Land of the Legged.

It was a plan full of potholes, but it was the only plan she had.

Shifting her body weight onto one side so she could try to prop herself upright, Molly fought the urge to grunt. Then, slipping her hand through the slim crack in the door, she felt around for something loose and fabricky.

No luck. The cheers got louder as the penguins reached the halfway point of their circuit.

*Quick*, Molly thought, *before the parade ends and the kiosk person puts down their phone!*

Desperation mounting, she shoved her arm deeper into

the kiosk and finally found something soft and flowy. She grabbed on to it and pulled.

An almighty squeal erupted from the kiosk.

The door swung open, and Molly looked up at the girl whose apron she'd grabbed.

It was Felicity Davison.

# Look, a Penguin

Felicity's eyes widened. Her trout lips fell open. "What the..."

Molly held up her hands as though she were about to be arrested. "Felicity, please, don't—"

Opening her wooden mouth as wide as she could, Felicity let out an almighty scream. Thankfully, an emperor penguin had done a little trick jump right at that very moment, and the cheers all but drowned out the wail.

"W-what is this?" Felicity whispered fearfully, staring at Molly's stark white tail. "What *are* you? Is this some kind of joke?"

"Yes! It is!" Molly insisted. "That's exactly what it is. Margot put me up to it. You know Margot? My sister? She's big on pranks. Really big. And, erm, this is one of them. Gotcha!"

Felicity glared at Molly with a charming mix of hatred and distrust. "So the tail isn't real? You're just an idiot?"

Nodding enthusiastically, Molly replied, "The biggest idiot in Idiotsville." This was, at the very least, believable.

Felicity took a step toward Molly, who fought the urge to cower. She had to act casual, like this really *was* a silly prank. Otherwise, her fear would show Felicity the truth.

"But...but it looks real." Before Molly could stop her, Felicity bent down and touched the slippery tip of the tail with her manicured hand. She leaped back from its glistening scales with an "Arrrghhh!"

Molly's heart raced with fear. She couldn't let the world find out the truth about her double life as a mermaid. Not just because the thought made her convulse with horror and shame, but because her family had impressed on her the importance of keeping this quiet.

What would happen if she betrayed them? Would she be taken to mermaid prison and left to rot? Would she be thrown to the piranhas and ripped to shreds?

Or, worst of all, would her family be disappointed in her?

As Felicity's yells got louder, Molly panicked. She needed to shut her up, fast. And for that, she needed a distraction.

The penguins were marching back toward the enclo-sure, right past the opening where Molly lay wedged between the kiosk and the fence. Without thinking, she grabbed the nearest baby penguin and pulled it into her nook.

It barked.

Well, it was more of a chirp or a honk than a bark. But still. The penguin frantically flapped its flippers, trying to escape.

"Look," Molly said, deadpan. "A penguin."

At a loss for what to do next, Molly put the poor penguin in her lap, thinking maybe it would enjoy the sensation of scales and feel more at home.

*Oh God, penguins eat fish, don't they?* What if it tried to eat her?

Instead, Molly picked it up again and held it in the air, like Rafiki holding up baby Simba in *The Lion King*.

"A penguin," she reiterated.

Felicity stared at her in horror, flapping her hands much like the abducted penguin. "Oh my *God*, what are you doing? Let him go! Let him go!"

"No," Molly retorted, although keeping hold of the squirming bird was becoming increasingly difficult. They were heavier—and slimier—than they looked. "Not unless you promise not to tell anyone."

Molly felt sort of bad about this. She hadn't meant to use the penguin for hostage negotiations, but that was just the way the situation turned out.

"OK! OK, whatever!" Felicity begged. "Please, just let him go before you hurt him."

"How do you know it's a him?" Molly asked sincerely, but Felicity reached for the walkie-talkie tucked into her belt loop, seconds away from calling security. "OK, OK," Molly added hastily. "Here you go."

She placed the penguin back on the ground, and he waddled away happily. He joined the back of the parade as though nothing had happened. Molly found herself feeling jealous of him.

Felicity collapsed against the doorframe of the kiosk, rubbing her eyes in disbelief. Mascara ended up smudged all down her cheeks. "I can't believe this... What? How? Mermaids aren't real. It—"

"But you promised not to tell anyone, remember?" Fear was building in Molly's chest. She didn't trust Felicity. Not one little bit. "You *just* promised. Please, Felicity."

"Or what?" Felicity snapped. "You'll keep kidnapping penguins?"

"Look, I know we don't get along—"

"It's not that we don't get along." Felicity twisted her face cruelly. "I just don't care about you at all. The *only* reason I know who you are is because of the deep fryer smell."

Something inside Molly snapped at that, and pure, hot anger flooded her veins. She clenched her fists so hard, her fingernails dug into her palms. There was something underneath the potent anger too. Something that twisted and coiled like a python in her gut.

Shame.

She was ashamed of who she was. Humiliated to her very core.

While she'd been embarrassed before, this was a whole new level. It was bone-deep shame. It was a part of her.

Molly looked up at Felicity, looked into her deep hazel eyes, and then something very strange happened.

Molly felt Felicity's shame too.

She felt the argument Felicity had had with her stepdad that morning. Felicity had told him she hated him, and she was ashamed of herself for that. He'd only been trying to help her plan her study schedule.

She felt the embarrassment of when Felicity's latest report came home and her mom saw how much her grades had dropped. She felt the fear of failing her classes and never leaving this tiny town.

She felt how Felicity saw herself when she looked in the mirror: like a scared little girl who just wanted to be perfect.

All this came flooding to Molly like a dam had burst. She couldn't understand why she'd never noticed any of this about Felicity before. It was written all over her face.

Felicity's eyes widened at Molly as though she could feel something odd happening too but didn't quite understand what it was.

That made two of them.

And then, beneath it all, Molly saw something more raw and jagged than everything else. The root cause of Felicity's shame.

Her mom was sick. Cancer.

*Oh no. Oh God.*

Molly's heart hurt. She wanted desperately to say something profound to Felicity. Something to let her know she understood that very particular sadness and fear.

However, Molly was not good with words, so instead, she said, "I'm sure your math grade will pick up if you buy Ms. Stavros a protractor."

Felicity's eyes narrowed. "What are you talking about?"

"Your grades. I'm sure you won't fail. And your stepdad knows you don't hate him really."

Felicity looked as though she might punch Molly in the mouth.

Molly's chest twisted. She hurt for Felicity. She knew how desperately painful it was to watch your family go through something so awful.

But why would her mom being ill make her feel...

ashamed? Because that was the overriding emotion she could feel from Felicity: shame. It didn't make sense.

Deep down, though, it made all the sense in the world. Because Molly had felt that way too.

"It's OK if you resent her, you know." Molly's voice was barely a whisper.

Felicity's expression grew even fiercer. She clenched her fist around her phone. "What did you just say to me?"

"Your mom." Molly swallowed hard. "My mom had cancer too. And it's OK to resent her for having it, even though you think it makes you a bad person. It doesn't. You're just...human." *Even though all signs point otherwise*, Molly added to herself.

"How do you know about my mom?" Felicity choked out. "Nobody knows. I made sure."

"I don't know," Molly admitted, and it was the truth. "I just had an inkling."

Felicity's face crumpled then, and she began to cry. "I don't know why I'm so angry with her about it. It's not like she *chose* to be sick."

"And yet now your entire life is *about* her being sick," Molly said softly. "It's all you can think about, and all the rest of your family can think about. It's ruined everything."

Rivers of snot dribbled into Felicity's kitchen table mouth. "I hate myself for it."

Molly nodded. She wanted to tell Felicity she *shouldn't* hate herself, that she couldn't help having those feelings, but she knew that wouldn't change anything. So instead, she said, "That's normal too. But it goes away, I promise."

Felicity sniffed and wiped her nose on the back of her wrist. "Your mom got better?"

Molly smiled then. "She got better. You know the skinny-dipping Ada told you about?"

Felicity's lips quirked, but not in a cruel way. "Yeah."

"That's my mom just…celebrating being alive. Reclaiming her body." *And giving her tail a little bit of a stretch.*

For the first time ever while thinking about her mom's skinny-dipping, Molly didn't feel ashamed or embarrassed. She felt proud of her tough, joyful mom. She felt grateful beyond words that she had beaten cancer. Watching a forty-year-old woman dance naked in the sea was a thousand times better than the alternative.

Felicity sat with this thought for a second. Molly watched the different emotions flicker across Felicity's face and wondered again how she'd never noticed them before. There was anger, then fear, then hope. Then anger again.

Was this her merpower? Tapping into people's emotions like a radio station she hadn't been able to reach until now?

Sniffing hard and setting her jaw in a defiant tilt, Felicity forced strength into her voice. "Don't you dare tell anyone. About my mom. I don't want people feeling sorry for me."

"Of course I w—"

"If you do, I'll tell the world about your...*thing*." She pointed at Molly's tail, but her earlier disgust had eased off.

Molly blinked, hardly daring to believe her luck. Felicity was willing to keep quiet about the tail if Molly kept Felicity's mom's secret. Which meant that if Felicity ever *did* tell anyone about the mermaid thing, she'd lose her leverage. Even though she was *technically* being blackmailed, this was kind of the best-case scenario.

Still, she didn't want Felicity to know how much of a win this was, so she pretended to consider the proposal deeply.

"And you'll get me out of here," Molly added, shaking now. "Without anyone seeing."

Felicity swallowed and nodded.

And that's the story of how Molly Seabrook was packed up in a T-shirt box and pushed out of a zoo in a seal-shaped wagon.

# The Strangest Merpower

**M**olly spent the whole drive back to Little Marmouth in a jittery state. Even though Ada hadn't seen anything, Molly was convinced she smelled like penguin. Surely, that was bound to raise some questions.

Thankfully, Ada was too busy ranting about Penalty Pete to notice.

When she got back to Kittiwake Keep, Molly was relieved to find Margot alone in her room. Once she'd confirmed that everything had gone all right with Eddie of the Ears—they gave him a gift voucher as thanks, and Molly texted him a huge thank-you—and that Aunt Maureen had not been roasted in a deep fryer, Molly started to fill Margot in on everything that had happened at the zoo.

*Everything*. Blackmail and all.

After Molly had finished, Margot sat in stunned silence. "Wow."

"Yup."

"That's...wow."

"Just saying wow a lot isn't going to help me here."

Margot started to French braid her unruly hair. "What do you want me to say?"

Molly flopped on to the bed and sighed. "That I'm not a terrible person."

"What?" Margot looked genuinely confused. "Why would you be a terrible person?"

Slowly, as though talking to a particularly idiotic garden snail, Molly said, "I blackmailed Felicity Davison using a mystery superpower."

Margot shrugged. "Technically, *she* blackmailed *you*."

"So...I shouldn't feel bad?"

"I don't know why you're asking me for validation. I'm not exactly the best judge of what's right and wrong. Once, I pranked an old man at work, and he peed himself."

"Margot! You said you had nothing to do with that!"

"I lied." Margot shrugged, twisting the final lock of hair and securing it with a tiny bobble. "See? Nobody's a good person all the time."

Molly chewed the dry skin around her thumbnail. "But we should still, like...try, no?"

"Yeah. Probably. OK, from now on, let's at least try to be good people." A wide grin. "Except for when Felicity Davison's in the room. Then I can't promise anything. Even with all that going on in her life, she still acts like she's begging to be smashed in the face with a water balloon."

They both cackled then—real, deep belly laughs that melted away some of the leftover tension from the zoo. Molly was very grateful for Margot in that moment.

"But seriously, though," Molly said once she'd finally calmed down. "I don't understand my merpower."

"Me neither."

"What even...is it?" Molly had practically gnawed her thumb down to the bone at this point. "It was just... I could feel her emotions."

"So you can read minds? That's awesome."

Molly shook her head. "Not quite. I couldn't tell exactly what she was thinking or, like, what she'd had for lunch. Just the emotions she was feeling. Especially shame."

"Give it time. Merpowers become stronger the more you use them. Like a muscle. Maybe one day, you'll be able to read minds properly."

The thought sent a dark thrill up Molly's spine. But before

she could ask any more questions, Melissa came waltzing into the room. She was still wearing her chip-shop uniform, which was stained with flour and batter. Combined with her cocoa body spray, she smelled like a deep-fried Mars bar.

"What are you guys talking about?"

At the same time, Molly and Margot both said, "Nothing."

To Molly's great surprise, Melissa's shoulders slumped, and a sad expression flitted across her face. "Why do you always do that when I walk into the room?"

Margot looked nervously at Molly. "Do what?"

"Stop talking." Melissa stared at the ground. "Act like Aunt Maureen's just appeared in the doorway."

Margot winced. "Well...you can be a little...Auntie-ish."

"That's not very nice, Margot," Melissa chastised. "You should really be nicer to people."

It would have been very easy to point out that Melissa had just proven Margot right, but Molly decided not to cause World War III. She was a little tired. "Funnily enough, we were just saying that."

Melissa gave her a weak smile. "How was the zoo? It's nice that you and Ada are friends again."

At the sound of Ada's name, Molly's stomach churned uncomfortably. "Mmm."

"What? What's wrong?"

Molly sighed deeply. "It's just... It's hard, having to keep the mermaid thing a secret from her. I mean, I'm not even sure I *want* her to know. She'd think I was an even bigger freak than ever. I just hate knowing that if she did find out somehow, I'd get us all in trouble."

Melissa nodded sagely, like a middle-aged woman. "It's a burden we all have to bear." There was a strange little beat in which Melissa glanced at the ground once again. "The trick is not to get too close to anyone."

Molly stared out the window at the night sky. It was clear, and the stars twinkled over the ocean. "What happens if...the humans do find out?" It felt strange using the word *humans* as though it wasn't a group she was part of.

Climbing into her bathrobe, Margot mumbled, "We'll all be sent back to Meire. All of us."

"Meire?" Molly asked, surprised that the answer didn't involve being mauled by piranhas. "The old mermaid queendom?"

"Yup."

"But I thought you said it was overrun with plastic and pollution."

"And poop," Margot pointed out.

"It is," Melissa agreed, a prim look on her face. She didn't like discussing bodily functions, which Molly found difficult to wrap her head around. "Being sent back to Meire would be a death sentence. That's why we have to be so strict about keeping it a secret. It's for our own good, Molly."

Molly's stomach twisted and turned. "And if we were sent to Meire, we'd never be allowed back home?"

"No. Never."

Molly's heart sank at the thought of never coming back to Little Marmouth. Never seeing Ada again or eating sea marbles or serving onion rings to Cute Steve. No more crooked lighthouse or dressing up as a haddock. Even though some of those things drive her up the wall she would really, really miss them if they were taken away from her.

Maybe her life wasn't as horrible as she thought it was.

# The Good Ship Haddock

A few days later, Mom and Myla returned from Prescott University. Mom went straight to check up on the chip shop—probably to make sure Margot hadn't burned it down in her absence—while Myla went straight up to her bedroom at the very top of Kittiwake Keep. None of this was particularly unusual, but Molly found herself feeling a little dejected. She'd really been looking forward to seeing her mom and sister.

After everything that had gone down over the last month, Molly had promised herself that she wouldn't take her family—or her life—for granted. So while her gut instinct was to leave Myla to her studying, she decided to go up there for the first time in years. She remembered how much she appreciated Myla coming to see her on the night of her first transformation and hoped her big sister would feel the same today.

Tapping softly on the open door, Molly said, "Hey."

Myla, who was predictably sitting at her desk by the porthole window, turned around. "Molly! What a surprise." She blinked through her glasses. "Is everything OK?"

"Of course!" Molly smiled. "I just wondered how your interview went."

Myla nodded. "It was OK, I think. Some unexpected questions, but I fudged through the answers."

Molly stared at her. "I never thought I would hear you, Myla Seabrook, admit to fudging through anything."

"I fudge through a lot of things." Myla laughed. She adjusted a book on her shelf that was slightly out of place. "You think all the school stuff comes easy to me?"

"Uh, yes. You're a supergenius."

Myla scoffed. "Only because I study a lot. I find it as difficult as anyone else."

This genuinely surprised Molly. She thought Myla was just naturally Einstein-y. "I didn't know that."

Myla shrugged. "You've never asked me."

There was an uncomfortable pause. Molly thought of purple-tailed Amy and how hurt Margot was that Myla had kept her love life a secret. But really, it was more the case that they never asked Myla about her life. They just left her here alone at the top of the Keep, never bothering to ask what was going on with her.

"I'm sorry," Molly mumbled.

"Don't be silly," Myla said too quickly.

"No, really. I am. I should ask you things more often."

Myla tucked her legs up under herself. "I'm just as guilty. I know we don't talk much, Mol, but with you and Margot being so close... I just feel like I'm interrupting sometimes."

There was a sadness in her voice that Molly hated hearing. Especially since she'd heard the very same sadness in Melissa's voice when she'd told them she didn't like the fact that they stopped talking when she was around.

Molly thought of how left out she felt when Ada was hanging around with Felicity and the popular group and wondered if that was how her sisters felt around her and Margot. It was a horrible thought. She never wanted anyone to feel like that, especially the people she loved. Because she did. She loved her sisters. Even though seventy-five percent of them were a pain in the tail.

"Please don't think that," Molly said softly. She swallowed hard. "Especially with you going away next year. I want to spend more time with you."

To Molly's surprise, Myla started to cry. Not big, rollicking sobs, just a gentle trickle of tears. She sniffed and wiped her eyes on her sleeve. "That's really sweet. Come here."

Hugging Myla for the first time in forever, Molly couldn't help but shed a tear herself.

ℓ·ℓ·ℓ

After school the next day, Molly finally got the chance to sit down with her mom and talk through everything that had happened. She left out the part about being blackmailed by Felicity, because she didn't want to admit someone knew about her tail, but she *did* confess to discovering her strange merpower. Mom was just as confused as Margot had been.

Mom stirred a spoonful of sugar into her black coffee. "I wish I could explain it, kiddo, but I've never heard of anything like it."

"Great. I knew I was a freak."

Mom laughed at this. "We're all freaks. You're right at home." There was a pause as she sipped, then smiled warmly. "But we'll figure it out together, Mol. I promise. Now get dressed. You're needed on the Good Ship Haddock."

The December afternoon was cold, and for once, Molly was not sweating in her haddock suit. In fact, it was the beginning of a rather pleasant evening, with the gushing and fizzing of waves on the shore, the cawing of the seagulls overhead, and the kaleidoscope of red and orange and pink as the sun set over the sea.

As she watched Ada frolicking on the beach with Penalty Pete, Cute Steve, and Felicity, she found herself getting jealous once again. She wanted to be spending her evenings laughing in the sand and having rock-skipping competitions, not handing out leaflets and worrying about whether or not she was about to transform.

But for some reason, the feeling of being left out didn't sting quite as much as before. Knowing this life could be taken from her in the blink of an eye made her appreciate it all the more. She was genuinely grateful for her weird family. Her weird, skinny-dipping mom and her messy, complicated, wonderful sisters. Who, you know, also happened to be mermaids.

As Molly was thrusting handfuls of leaflets at locals who probably had a thousand identical leaflets stuffed in their kitchen drawers, Ada and her new crew climbed the steps back on to the boardwalk and started walking in Molly's direction. They all laughed at something Cute Steve said, and for a split second, Molly worried they were mocking her.

The familiar burn of shame stung in her cheeks. She was wearing a *haddock* suit. In front of the love of her life and the most popular girl in school. *Who knew she was a mermaid.*

At least she'd remembered to put on some of the lipstick Ada had gotten her for her birthday. Although she suspected she might have done it wrong. There was a funny taste in her mouth. Maybe it wasn't supposed to go all the way inside your lips.

For an agonizing moment, she half expected her friend to ignore her and walk straight past, but to her enormous relief, Ada stopped and waved. "Hey, Mol. How's it going?"

Ada acknowledging their friendship in front of the Populars made her beam like a lighthouse. "Good, you?"

"Fine. Hey, you know C— Steve, right?"

Cute Steve nodded in her direction. "How's it goin'?"

"This is Pete, and this is Felicity."

Felicity gave Molly the tiniest of smiles. "Hi."

Molly smiled back. Reflex made her want to say something snarky, but knowing what she did about Felicity's mom—*feeling* the pain for herself—stopped her in her tracks. The wave of sympathy was so powerful, it almost took her breath away.

"Hey," she mumbled. "Nice to meet you."

Then the two girls nodded at each other, so subtly nobody else noticed, and a burst of warmth rocketed through Molly's chest. It really did feel better to be nice.

In the back of her mind, she briefly worried what would happen if news naturally got out about Felicity's mom. Molly would completely lose her leverage, and there would be nothing to stop Felicity from telling the world about Molly being a mermaid. This whole setup was a ticking time bomb.

Maybe she could try to befriend Felicity for real. She didn't seem that bad, underneath her cool-girl facade. And Molly could definitely relate to a lot of what she was going through—the sick mom, the poor grades, feeling totally at odds with herself.

It was certainly worth a try.

"I like your teeth," Molly blurted out. Then, as though it would make her ridiculous statement *less* weird, she added, "They are very straight and white. Shiny."

*Shiny. Just...why, Molly?*

But Felicity only smiled again. "Thanks. That's sweet."

Cute Steve nodded at the leaflets in Molly's fin. "So you have to get rid of all those flyers, huh?"

"Yup. Our family basically murders an entire rain forest every month just to get these printed."

"Gimme a handful. I'll ask my boss if we can have some on the ice cream counter."

Molly couldn't quite believe it. He was offering to do her, Molly Seabrook, a favor! "Thanks, Steve," she said, as calmly as she could muster.

This was, quite frankly, an astonishing turn of events.

She was talking to Cute Steve, and not once had she uttered the words "onion rings." Or "glumph," for that matter.

Maybe this was it. Maybe this was the start of her journey into the popular group.

Right at that second, Minnie darted out of the shop and yanked her by the hand. Well, fin.

"Molly-macaroni," she asked excitedly. "Did you have a nice poop earlier?"

Then again, maybe not.

# Acknowledgments

Working on this series has been so much fun that I don't think it would be fair to call it work—in no small part thanks to my amazing publishing team, who have been a dream since day one. Thank you to my literary agent, Suzie Townsend (I'm sorry for making you rep a mermaid book), the rest of the New Leaf family, and of course Team Egmont: Ali, Liz, Siobhan, Olivia, Sarah, Hilary, Laura, Amy, Janene, Susila, and Melissa. You're all brilliant.

My incredible writing friends: especially Emma Theriault, Sasha Alsberg, and Francina Simone. Operation world domination is a go.

My real human pals (because all writers are witches and cyborgs): Mum, Dad, Jack, Gran, Toria, Nic, Hannah, Lauren, Lucy, Hilary, Steve, and Spike. My dog, Obi, even though the reading lessons aren't going so well. And Millie, the best mermaid I know.

And finally, to my husband, Louis. I love you. I apologize if this book brings shame to the Kirkpatrick name, but really, you knew what you were getting into when you said "I do."

# About the Author

Laura Kirkpatrick is part mermaid, part children's author living in northern England. Her favorite things are white chocolate, beach walks with her puppy, and hiding her tail from prying humans. In addition to her fiction, Laura is a journalist and screenwriter.

Don't miss more of
Molly's mermaid adventures
in *Don't Tell Him I'm a Mermaid*!

# DON'T TELL HIM
## I'M A
# MERMAID